The
Awakening

Other works by this author:

Final Flight of the Ranegr
The Starlight Lancer
Path of a Hero
The Cursed Jewel
Metanoia
The Star Warriors

Find them online at
https://www.cscooper.com.au/books

The
Awakening

C. S. Cooper

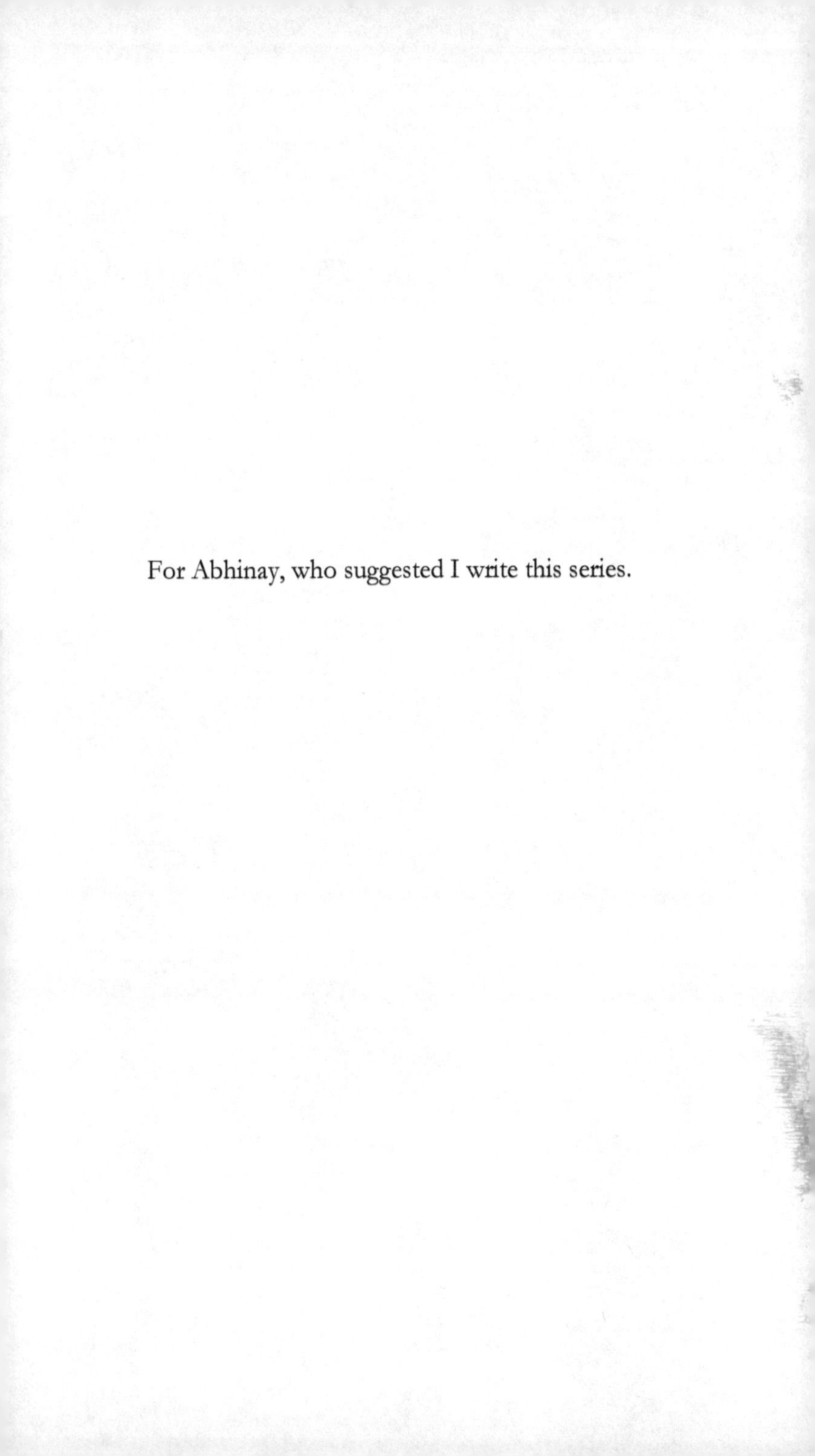

For Abhinay, who suggested I write this series.

CONTENTS

Acknowledgements

I acknowledge the artist group, CLAMP, whose manga inspired this story. I also thank the people who read my novel, *Final Flight of the Ranegr*. Since you were so intrigued by *The AXOM Saga*, and requested paperback copies, here you go. Then, there are my parents and family, who encouraged me to publish it.

1 | Going Viral

The whole of Tokyo felt the bite of winter's chill as a full moon loomed over Tokyo Tower. Even the slightest breeze felt like a gust of wind from a freezer. Only one girl in the entire city could be concerned with something other than the weather.

That girl bounded across rooftops like Superman, leaping tall buildings in a single bound. But she wasn't from Krypton, or even from Venus. She was just a regular girl, *with magical powers*. The ethereal wings faded from her ankles as she landed gracefully on a rooftop in view of the brightly illuminated Tokyo Tower. Her pink cape and costume wafted in time with the bangs of her neck length chestnut mane, which she drew back over her ears as she gazed fixedly at the latticework of beams and trusses that made up the tower.

"Sakura, there it is," said the flying teddy bear floating beside her. He pointed toward the base of the tower, and the girl grinned excitedly.

Suddenly, a key floated before her, and she uttered with purpose an incantation:

> *Key who conceals the Magic of Shadow,*
> *Ye who is more than ye seems:*
> *I command thee to bestow*
> *The power ye deems.*

Let us fulfil our vow
In time's great streams … Release!

With a flash the key became a pink, bird-head staff, which she grabbed before she leapt off the roof. A Card flew out in front of her, and she cried, "Give me wings! Fly!" The Card dematerialised in a flash of light that formed resplendent wings upon the girl's back. Gravity lost its hold on her as she swooped out of her nose-dive and sped toward the tower. The little creature hiding within snarled at her approach and attempted to escape along the railing. Sakura's little teddy bear partner was too fast for it, and cut off its escape. The rabbit bared its fangs defensively, but was spooked when Sakura landed on the boardwalk and brandished her staff.

"Jump Card! That's enough mischief!" Sakura shouted sternly, as if she were Julie Andrews in a Disney movie. The creature withdrew from her, darted around her teddy bear partner, and made a beeline for the other side of the tower.

"Kero! Keep it moving that way!" Sakura ordered.

"Roger!" returned Kero and flew after the thing. Sakura sprinted the other way, darting off the railing so as not to lose her momentum. She drew two more Cards from her pocket, and smirked confidently as she screeched to a stop at the next corner. There was the rabbit, trembling as it assumed a defensive posture.

"Wind and forest, make thy currents and vines binding chains," she murmured to the Cards, before striking them with her wand. "Windy! Wood!"

From nowhere, a forest of vines and strident gusts enveloped the irate rabbit and it snarled angrily. Though it struggled and screeched, the winds and vines held it tightly as Sakura approached. With a twirl of her wand, she roared, "Return to thine intended form, Clow Card!"

With a last acquiescent wail, the rabbit dematerialised into a shimmering rainbow light, which swirled about her as it coalesced into another Card. The picture emblazoned upon the Card showed a portrait of her captured rabbit, with the words 'The Jump' adorned below it in classic European calligraphy. The girl pocketed the Cards that were the source of her magical power, twirled her magic wand about her, and gave a triumphant pose to the camera.

The whole class roared with applause, no one applauding louder than the jet-black-haired girl behind the camera. Her eyes glimmered with starlight as she imagined all the Oscars her actress was soon to win. That actress, whose winning pose was still frozen at the end of the YouTube video, stood beside her, with her palms buried in her face.

"Tomoyo! I can't believe you uploaded this," said Sakura, her face absolutely blood red with embarrassment and concern.

"Oh, but I had to, my Dear Sakura," said Tomoyo with more enthusiasm than a writer holding his first published novel. "This is your debut as a film star!" That only made the very shy Sakura cringe.

"Yeah, Sakura," said the girl in front of the laptop on which the video was playing. She adjusted her glasses and added, "You and Tomoyo could be a team! Make awesome movies and win tonnes of awards! Man, I wish I were as imaginative as you two were. My fantasy stories are terrible."

"I'm not movie star material, Naoko," Sakura replied as she hunched, wanting nothing more than to disappear into the floor.

Another girl with pigtails, whose name was Chiharu, intoned, "Don't be ridiculous! You've already gone viral!"

As Sakura withdrew from the laptop and hid behind Tomoyo, the boy next to Chiharu raised his finger and said in a very matter-of-fact voice, "Do you know why they're called 'viral videos?'"

Chiharu cringed and moaned, "Oh, Takeshi, don't

start!"

Oh, but he *did* start: "In the olden days, viruses were what made people sick. They were carried by pictures, you see. The Ancient Egyptians used viral pictures to safeguard the Pharaoh's tombs. And when YouTube got started, they had a lot of problems, because videos would carry viruses, just like the Ancient Egyptian pictures, and make people sick. But because all the kids wanted to get out of going to school, they'd all watch them, get sick, and got to have days off."

Chiharu, having reached her limit, proceeded to swat Takeshi over the head. The boy's grin widened as the girl angrily berated him, and Sakura's face turned pale.

"Tomoyo! Take the video down. I don't want to make people sick!" she cried.

The group stared at her bewildered.

"Sakura, he's joking," said Chiharu very slowly.

"Of course I am, Sakura," said Takeshi with a grin. "The *real* reason they're called Viral Videos is because the video was invented by a man named Stratford von Viralshire."

Chiharu's blow almost knocked him out cold.

* * *

Sakura's video was the talk of the school. In the locker room, she noticed kids watching it on their phones, their mouths agape with wonder at the quality of the special effects and sound production. There were even a few requests for a feature length video, which made Sakura's cheeks so hot they could fry an egg, and Tomoyo's head swim with ambitious ideas.

Sakura ringed her hands as if they were saturated by her own embarrassment. She kept doing that all the way home, while Tomoyo excitedly brainstormed all her ideas, speaking at a million words per second.

"Tomoyo! I don't think we should be making videos like that," exclaimed Sakura. "What if people find out?"

"Find out what?" asked Tomoyo, genuinely oblivious.

"That you're not *that* good at special effects," Sakura whispered.

"Pah! No one would think that!" replied Tomoyo. "When it comes to making my Dear Sakura a star, nothing is impossible for Tomoyo Daidouji!"

"Jump didn't exactly like pretending to be captured a second time," Sakura sighed.

"I'm sure he had fun doing it," Tomoyo insisted.

Sakura gazed up at her house, approaching on the right, and mumbled, "I can think of someone else who won't be too impressed with the video."

The pair discarded their shoes at the entrance to the house and crept into the kitchen. Sakura turned to a picture of a beautiful Japanese woman with flowing hair and said, "I'm home, Mum!"

A Caucasian man in his late thirties stood over the stove, and greeted them with a smile over his shoulder.

"Welcome home, Sakura," said the man as he set the spaghetti sauce on simmer. "I see my little girl has become a movie star." He beamed proudly, which only made Sakura's shyness worse. Before she could respond, Tomoyo spoke up.

"Oh dear! I completely forgot," she exclaimed. "I should have asked permission before I uploaded a video of Sakura. Forgive me, Mister Kinomoto." She gave a low bow, which Sakura eyed with a raised eyebrow.

No thought to ask my permission, she wondered internally.

"Not at all, Miss Daidouji," replied the man. "I'm glad you and Sakura have a common interest. And it was a very exciting video too."

"Wasn't it just?" exclaimed Tomoyo. "And it's only the first in the series, Mister Kinomoto."

Sakura was mortified.

First in the series?

"Well, I'll look forward to it," said Mister Kinomoto. "Sakura, just remember your old Dad when you're world-famous!"

Sakura had had enough, and quickly changed the subject, "Well, Tomoyo and I have a lot of homework to do. So we'll go do it in my room." She grabbed Tomoyo's hand and dragged her up to her bedroom. Before she had any chance to push away the idea of being a film star, a voice with a thick Kansai[1] accent perked up. It came from the winged gold-furred teddy bear on Sakura's desk, and with a deep, accusatory tone it said, "You uploaded the video?"

"Yes, we did!" replied Tomoyo.

The teddy bear suddenly leapt to its feet and bellowed with joy, "Wahoo! I'm an Internet icon!"

Tomoyo joined hands with the teddy bear and said, "Let us make our Sakura a star!"

"Make me a star!" retorted the teddy bear with a twitch of his dish-shaped ears.

"Kero! Not you too," lamented a face-palming Sakura.

Kero floated over to the girl and patted her on the head, "Don't be shy, my master. You looked so insanely cool in the video." Sakura glared at the floating bear, who quickly added with a triumphant cross of his arms, "Only by reflecting my unadulterated coolness, though. And when you capture the Earthy and Firey Cards, I'll be able to unleash my true form. I'll be so unbelievably cool, Jack Black'll make a movie about me!"

Tomoyo and Kero began their brainstorming while Sakura tried her best to disappear into the deepest corner of her bedroom. She gazed at her two friends chatting and plotting, and her mind drifted to a month ago.

* * *

Sakura frowned as she walked through Chiyoda City. She gazed down at her phone, which bore a list of bookstores in the area. These were not regular Japanese bookstores,

---

1   Rather than an accent, Kansai is a dialect of Japanese spoken in the area
     including Osaka city.

but rather antique shops. Most of the list had been crossed off, and there was just one more to check.

"Sakura, I think you're going a bit too far here," said Tomoyo as she yawned. Bags full of sewing equipment and materials weighed her down, and she was growing tired.

"I want to make sure I get Naoko a good gift," Sakura insisted. "She got me such a nice make-up set for my fifteenth, and I want something that … you know, matches her interests."

"Why are we looking at English bookstores?" asked Tomoyo. "I know you speak English, but poor Naoko won't."

Sakura sighed, "I know. I just keep thinking, maybe I'll find something fantasy or occult or whatever in one of these places. Naoko loves that kind of thing."

"Ah! My Sakura is so sweet and conscientious," chirped Tomoyo.

They found the last one on the list, *Ogawa Tosho*, between a hairstylist and an alleyway. It seemed totally unassuming, given what lay inside.

"I'll just be a minute," said Sakura. Tomoyo walked a little further ahead to look at the menu on the *Siddique* restaurant two stores down.

The inside of the bookstore smelled musty, as to be expected of old books. The old man in charge of the store greeted her with a warm smile, and adjusted his brown baseball cap as she approached.

"I'm looking for something that looks … sort of," Sakura struggled to find the words. "Occulty?"

"Occulty?" rasped the man in a Kansai accent. "That some new thing today?"

"I don't know," said Sakura, slumping her shoulders. "I've got a friend who likes mystery, fantasy, and the occult. I thought I might find a book here she'd like."

"Ah! I think I understand," replied the man. He led Sakura deeper into the shop. From behind one of the larger bookcases, he pulled out a cardboard box that looked far too heavy for him. Sakura helped him heft the box onto the table. Inside were dozens of books, with covers of varied yet faded colours. "Here we are," said the man. "I've had this collection of books for years. There's stuff from all over the world here. Donated from archaeologists and collectors."

Sakura began to sift through the books. Some of them had some detailed decorations on them, with titles written in Latin, English, French, and even some Chinese and Hindi (she assumed). While looking at a book with Tamil writing impressed in peeling gold, she absentmindedly reached into the box and touched a book covered in loose cloth. It caught her attention, and she picked it up.

"Ah, that's a good one," said the man with a glimmer to his eye. "Go on, open it."

Sakura unfurled the cloth, revealing the elaborately decorated book within. Gold filigree adorned the cover, and the same of silver covered the back, over which sat a glimmering symbol of the moon. The front bore a golden lion, its mane shimmering in the flickering light of the bookshop. Sakura ran her fingers over the engraved words 'The Clow' upon the front cover, and it gave her excited chills.

"Is this some kind of spell book?" asked Sakura.

"I dunno," said the man with a shrug. "I had that for years back in Osaka. Someone donated it to my store there, who got it from someone else in Taiwan. They said it belonged to a powerful magician." Sakura shot him a grin, and the man chuckled, "I know, crazy, huh? But I never found a key for the lock, so I dunno what's in there."

Sakura looked to the side of the book and saw the keyhole over the clasp. It held the book shut tightly. It was truly mysterious and beautiful, and the story to go with it would certainly delight Naoko. But, before Sakura could seal the deal, she hesitated.

"I think this is a bit too expensive for me," she

mumbled. "Look at how beautiful it is. It should be in an art exhibit or something."

"I've offered it to galleries, but they just ignore it," sighed the man. "Something about it not being post-modern enough, whatever that means." Sakura continued to grimace. "Tell ya what, what's your budget for this present?" asked the man.

"Five thousand is my absolute limit," said Sakura.

"How does four sound?" asked the man with a warm smile.

"Really?" exclaimed Sakura, her eyes bugging out.

"Girl, it's just collecting dust here," said the man. "This friend of yours loves mystery, so she'll appreciate it way more than the box here."

With a grin, Sakura handed over the money and wrapped the book in its cloth. She felt it added to the mysteriousness of the gift. With a grateful bow, she bade the shop owner farewell and headed back to meet Tomoyo. She spent the remainder of her budget on some snacks for her and her friend, and they went home.

In Sakura's bedroom, she unfurled the cloth and showed Tomoyo the book.

"How wonderful!" exclaimed Tomoyo. "This is ... I can't explain it. I think you went overboard on this present, Sakura. Naoko might be embarrassed by such a gift."

"It was only four thousand yen," said Sakura.

"Even so, it looks like it should be worth millions," mumbled Tomoyo. Sakura related the story the shopkeeper told her about the book. "Okay, Naoko will love this," said Tomoyo.

"Okay, let's wrap it," said Sakura.

While Tomoyo grabbed the scissors, wrapping paper, and tape from the bag, Sakura dusted off the book. She wanted to make it look presentable for her friend. As she ran her hand over it, the filigree seemed to leap out at her. It's myriad tints of gold and silver looked to her eyes like every shade of sunlight and moonshine. Then she gazed at the clasp on the side, and wondered what secrets it guarded. Softly, she brushed her finger over the keyhole.

Ting!

A sound echoed through the room, as if someone had struck a cup made of crystal. Sakura blinked in shock, as the clasp flicked open. Tomoyo looked over, equally surprised.

"What did you do?" she asked.

"Nothing, I just touched the lock and it opened," said Sakura. They exchanged glances before Sakura cautiously opened the book. There were no pages within. The inner cover was filled with writing neither Tomoyo nor Sakura could read. Where there would normally have been pages, there was only a cradle containing a stack of red tarot Cards. A golden glyph of the sun, partnered with a silver moon on the side, adorned the Cards.

Sakura edged her hand to it, and felt her fingertip tingle. The top-most Card felt warm to the touch. Gingerly, she lifted it out of the cradle.

"Cards?" mumbled Tomoyo. She saw the other side of the Card and said, "Wow, it's beautiful artwork."

Sakura turned it around to study it. The image was indeed beautiful. The woman resembled a spirit, her elegant dress taking the shape of a gust of wind.

"What does it say on the bottom?" asked Tomoyo.

Sakura looked down to the nameplate at the bottom of the Card, and read it aloud.

"Windy," she said.

The Card flashed. Tomoyo, the wrapping paper, their bags, the pencils on the desk, even the quilt on Sakura's bed, was thrown back by a fierce gust of wind. Sakura shrieked in panic as she looked around. She realised she was in the eye of a violent tornado, localised entirely within her bedroom. Sakura watched flabbergasted as her room turned into an absolute mess. She cried in horror upon realising she'd dropped the book, spilling the other Cards.

The wind whipped them from the floor and spun them about her. Then the Cards flew through her open window, and vanished into the sky.

The wind died as suddenly as it had started. Tomoyo stood trembling with her back against the wall. Sakura looked back at her, equally shocked.

"What the heck?" they mumbled.

The book began to glow, and they scampered away in confusion. Sakura held on to Tomoyo in sheer fright. The silver moon on the back disintegrated into a puff of feeble light, which then vanished. The golden lion on the front dematerialised into a sphere of luminance, which slowly morphed into the form of a winged teddy bear.

It looked at them a moment with a blank face.

"Wassap!" it suddenly bellowed.

Tomoyo and Sakura screamed in terror, and so did the teddy bear.

"Whacha screamin' for, huh?" yelled the teddy bear with a thick Kansai dialect.

"Tomoyo, it's talking," Sakura murmured.

The girls exchanged glances and pinched each other's cheeks. All it did was hurt them.

"It's not a dream," cried Tomoyo.

"'Course it ain't no dream, yo!" snapped the teddy bear.

"It's a talking teddy bear," mumbled Sakura. She grabbed the teddy bear and turned it around, pulling at its ears and legs. "What kind of tech is this? Where's the switch?" she cried frantically.

The teddy bear kicked itself out of her grip and snarled, "I ain't no toy! I'm Kerberus, the Beast of the Seal!" He raised his hand and the book hovered in the air toward him. He gestured to the empty book. "I'm the guardian of these, the Clow Cards!" He made a pose, as if expecting a round of applause, but received only silence. "What's the matter?" he said, meeting the girl's befuddled gazes. Then he looked at the book. His jaw dropped. "They're gone!" he cried. He took flight and flitted about the room, looking under every upturned plush toy, book, and piece of paper he could see. "Gone! Gone! Gone! Gone! Where are they?" he cried.

"Umm … I have one here," said Sakura shyly. She stood, Tomoyo cowering behind her, and held up the Windy Card still in her hand. The teddy bear beamed with relief and snatched the Card from her.

"Oh, Windy! Oh, I'm so glad you're fine," he wailed, embracing the Card as he would a long-lost sister. Then he looked at Sakura. "So, where are the others?"

"Well, you see," Sakura began sheepishly. "I opened the book and … well, I looked at the Card on the top of the deck. I read it, it said 'Windy,' but as soon as I said it … well, it made a big wind that wrecked my room. I was so frightened I dropped the other Cards, and they flew out the window." She strained to keep an innocent smile as she told her story. The teddy bear just kept a blank face.

"One moment, please," he said flatly. He then floated over to the bed, found Sakura's pillow, and jammed his face into it. His arms flailed about, and the girls could hear him yelling and screaming into the pillow.

The teddy bear then sat on the corner of Sakura's desk and proceeded to meditate. All he told them was, "I'm searching for the other Cards."

With no other explanation, Tomoyo and Sakura proceeded to clean up the bedroom. When it was finally in order, they sat on the bed and faced the strange creature.

"What did he say his name was?" asked Tomoyo.

"Kerberus," said Sakura. "Dad told me once. The gates of Hell are supposed to be guarded by a monster named Kerberus."

"Hell?" cried Tomoyo in a whisper. "Is this supposed to be some kind of demon?"

"I'm the hound of Hell," said the teddy bear, looking over his shoulder with a grin. Of course, his cute appearance and his non-threatening demeanour made the girls think he was joking. They gazed at each other.

"You don't look so scary," said Sakura.

"Rather than Kerberus, I'd say you're more a 'Kero,'" chuckled Tomoyo.

"I ain't no frog[2]," barked the teddy bear. He had a cute little pout that completely offset any threat the girls felt from him.

"We're just gonna call you Kero," said Sakura.

Kero crossed his arms and huffed, "You wouldn't say that if you saw my real form. It's super cool!"

"Can we see?" asked Tomoyo.

"Nope!" blurted Kero. "Since you've lost the Cards, I don't have much power."

"Aren't you supposed to be guarding them?" asked Sakura.

"Yeah, well, I kinda," Kero's voice dropped off.

"Kinda what?" asked Sakura.

"Fell asleep," muttered Kero.

Sakura's jaw dropped while Tomoyo burst into laughter.

"So much for a guardian," exclaimed Sakura.

"It's all in the past now!" bellowed Kero. "Besides, I didn't think someone with so much magical power would show up."

"Magical power?" asked Sakura.

"Yeah," blurted Kero. "Who opened the lock?" Tomoyo pointed at Sakura. "Then *you've* got magic powers. That's how you made that wind."

"*I* did that?" exclaimed Sakura. "How?"

"By activatin' the Windy Card," said Kero. "The Clow Cards were created by the supreme mage, Clow Reed. They're beings made of powerful elemental magic. Used wisely and they'd made the world a paradise. But used wrongly, they'd destroy it. He made me to guard the Cards until the day someone worthy of their power unlocked the book. That day comes, and you mess it all up by losing the

---

2   "Kero" is the Japanese onomatopoeia for a frog's croak.

Cards."

"*I* messed it up?" snapped Sakura. She thrust her finger at him. "You were sleeping on the job."

"You were playin' around with Windy," retorted Kero. "You lost 'em. Now they're runnin' wild. Who knows what calamity they'll make."

"Once again, Kero, you were delinquent," said Tomoyo, stepping up for her friend. "I think you should take responsibility in this. Sakura didn't know what she was doing."

Kero pouted, his arms folded defensively. He looked to the ground, and then looked up to Sakura. He held her gaze for a moment. Then he grinned.

"Let bygones be bygones," he chirped, floating up to her eye-level. "I didn't catch ya names?"

"I'm Sakura, and this is Tomoyo," said Sakura.

"Nice to meet ya," said Kero. He then paced in mid-air. "I'm the guardian, so I need to get the Cards back. But I can't sense them. And I won't be able to get them back alone. I was made by Clow to guard the Cards, not use 'em. Any chance you could help out?"

The girls nodded resolutely.

"It was partly my fault as well," said Sakura.

"Good," said Kero. He turned to Tomoyo. "Could you stand over there, real quick?"

Tomoyo stepped to the corner of the room, leaving Sakura standing in front of Kero alone. The teddy bear floated to the desk, and stood upon the Book of Clow. He held his arms up and softly mumbled, "Key of Shadows, a contractor stands before thee. A girl. Her name is Sakura." A dot of light shot out of the keyhole on the book's clasp and floated toward Sakura. It grew into the shape of a small key, a pink bird head its handle.

Kero began to chant.

> *Key of Shadows, more than ye seems,*
> *Thy contractor here, thy strength combined.*

The vow that awaits thee in time's great streams,
Let the contract be sewn, thy ties ever bind.

Then Kero roared, "Release!"

The key flashed and enveloped Sakura in mesmerising light. The key started to grow, until it became a metal staff with a jewelled bird head. It hovered in the air before the overwhelmed Sakura.

"Sakura, take it," exclaimed Kero.

Obediently, Sakura reached out and grasped the staff. Her arm tingled, much as when she touched the Windy Card. The light died down, and Sakura's room returned to normal.

"That's it!" exclaimed Kero. "I hereby proclaim you, *Cardcaptor Sakura!*"

Once again, Kero posed, expecting a round of applause. And once again, all he got was silence.

Sakura looked at him, and then to the staff in her hand.

"What just happened?" she asked.

"You are now under contract," chirped Kero. "You must use your magical powers, through that staff, to find the Cards and capture them."

"Magical powers!?" exclaimed Sakura. "I didn't ask for that! I didn't say you could give me magical powers!"

"I didn't give you anything," retorted Kero. "You already had them. I just gave you the Sealing Staff there so you could capture the Cards."

"I already ... had magic?" stammered Sakura.

"Since you were born," replied Kero. "You wouldn't've been able to open the Book of Clow if you didn't."

Sakura fell silent, overwhelmed by the news. Beside them, Tomoyo started to whine, her smile widening over her face. Her dam burst, and she flew into a paroxysm of joy. She threw her arms around Sakura and cried, "My Sakura is a Magic Girl!"

"Dang right, she is," chuckled Kero. "And she's gonna be cool doin' it."

"And look, I recorded that whole thing," exclaimed Tomoyo, brandishing her phone. She and Kero crowded the phone screen to watch the recording. Meanwhile, Sakura stepped back, her mouth agape, as she tried to process what had just happened.

Mystified, she wondered, *What did I just get into?*

* * *

Sakura came out of her reverie. Kero and Tomoyo were still at Sakura's desk, pouring over ideas for costumes and videos. It was just like when Sakura was first given the Shadow Key. She gazed at the Book of Clow in her hands.

Who'd have thought a fifteenth birthday present would lead to this, she wondered as she eyed the elaborately decorated book. *If these had been just regular Cards, Naoko would have loved them. But I just had to open it, and look inside, and then let this crazy critter trick me into this contract.*

She opened the book, and gazed at the four Cards nestled inside: Windy, Wood, Jump, and Fly. They seemed to gaze back at her and return her smile, which made her feel a little happier. She glanced at her desk, where Kero and Tomoyo were watching the video again. Sakura caught sight of the last shot, where she struck the winning pose Tomoyo had designed for her.

She couldn't help but smile giddily.

Oh, who am I kidding? Being Cardcaptor Sakura is awesome!

2 | Dreamweaver

There comes a time in everyone's life, in which their grudge toward their alarm clock reaches truly vengeful heights. Sakura almost reached that point one morning when the cursed device dragged her from a truly wonderful dream: one involving a kimono with floral patterns, fireworks, and takoyaki[3].

The sound of her father's voice dragged her the rest of the way from sleep. She threw on her uniform and brushed her hair.

"Y'know, ya wouldn't have a problem gettin' up if you went to sleep prop'ly," said Kero with a yawn.

Sakura glared at him getting under the covers of her bed and dozing. She said, "I don't want to hear that from someone who gets me up in the middle of the night to catch the Fly Card."

"Cardcaptor duties trump sleep," Kero droned half asleep.

Sakura plopped down on the bed next to the living stuffed animal and said, "What about you, who plays my big brother's video games until one in the morning?"

"Games trump guardian duties," replied Kero.

Her father's voice called her down, and she abandoned her friendly argument with Kero. She bade her mother's

---

3   Japanese fried octopus balls.

picture good morning, and sat opposite her brother. The moment she made eye contact and saw that plotting glimmer in his eyes, she shot him a suspicious glare.

"What's with all the rampaging?" mumbled the seventeen year old.

"I wasn't rampaging, Touya! I was just walking normally!" retorted Sakura.

"And practicing Kansai ventriloquy?" said Touya with a snide grin. "Seriously, when you walk around, it's like a crazy *kaiju*[4] is stamping around."

Sakura stomped her way toward her brother.

"I am not a kaiju!" she bellowed. Touya taunted her, and she charged into his palm, thrashing and hitting nothing but air.

"Now, now, don't roughhouse around the table," said their father as he set out the plates of food.

Sakura ate her fill, but took a little too long to prise the fat off her bacon. She knew her father went to a lot of effort to cut the fat away, but there was still quite a bit.

"I need to make sure I'm not too heavy for gymnastics practice this afternoon," she said.

When they were finished, their father bussed the plates. Sakura donned her rollerblades and joint guards, and followed Touya who rode on his bike. They turned a corner down the street onto the promenade. Sakura's eyes bugged out at the cherry blossom trees in full bloom. It'd been a warm March, so the flowers had come out early. She almost decided to skip school just to look at the flowering trees.

Oh, I can't wait for the next Ennichi[5] festival, she thought in a delighted daze.

A near-trip drew her attention back to the road. Her brother slowed as they drew near to a figure waiting on the footpath. From a distance, Sakura could see he was a boy

---

4   Japanese for Strange Beast, often referring to characters such as Godzilla.
5   A festival held in the summer.

about as tall as Touya, wearing the same uniform as her brother. When they came to a stop, Sakura barely took note of Touya bumping fists with the boy. She didn't even hear her brother introducing his new friend.

All she saw was this gorgeous, strapping young man. A flurry of sparkles, flowers, and love-hearts bordered her vision as her brain's internal iPod played 'Dreamweaver' by Gary Wright.

The boy of my dreams, screamed her inner voice.

The boy's teeth twinkled as he smiled and held his hand out to introduce himself. She took his hand, the touch electrifying the nerves running up her arms, as she said, "Nice to meet you! I'm Sa-moto Kino-kura!"

"You're sleep talking again, Kaiju!" said Touya with a roll of his eyes. His friend chuckled, which combined with the utterance of that hated nickname spurred Sakura to deftly punch her brother in the side. Touya did his best to hide his tears as the boy said, "I mustn't have said it right. My name is Yukito Tsukishiro."

"Mister Tsukishiro! What a lovely name!" droned Sakura in a smitten trance.

"Please call me Yukito," replied the boy with a warm smile. Then he suddenly had a realisation and said, "Hey, I've seen your Cardcaptor videos. You're an actor?"

"Oh, only in my spare time," replied Sakura gauchely, though she tried to throw off an air of humility. "They're something I do with my friends."

"You're great in them! I can see you becoming a real star someday," said Yukito with an excited smile.

At that, Sakura said flatly, "It's all my ideas. I do the concepts, the visual effects, the acting, the makeup, and the camera work!"

While Sakura talked up her contributions to the videos, Touya sniffed back his tears. He eventually broke in and said, "In case you were too busy being a zombie, Yuki here transferred to my school a month ago."

"I'm so glad to have met your brother and you," said

Yukito. "It's a little bothersome being in a new town and it's great to have some friends."

"I'm glad to meet you," said Sakura with a smile. Maintaining that smile, she shot her brother the evils and added, "If only Touya had introduced you sooner."

Touya finally brought up the time, and the three set back on the path to their schools. The boys' school was a bit further ahead from Sakura's, and the poor girl was forced to watch the back of Yukito's head as it moved away from her. The boy smiled over his shoulder and tossed a wrapped candy from his pocket. Sakura caught it, and subsequently liquefied.

"Ah! Yukito Tsukishiro! Wedding bell're gonna chime!" she intoned with a dazed smile.

Tomoyo appeared at the school gate just before the bell toll to see Sakura still in her rollerblades, humming 'Doo-wah-diddy.' She whipped out her phone and started recording. Sakura saw her friend and blurted, "Tomoyo! I am in love with that guy, and if I don't marry him then my life is meaningless!"

Tomoyo grabbed her hands, an overjoyed expression plastered over her face.

"You've found your Number One? Oh, Sakura, this is so wonderful!" she exclaimed. She suddenly whipped out her DSLR camera and snapped picture after picture of Sakura's loving gaze directed at the wrapped lolly.

Sakura hummed whatever romantic earworms buzzed about in her head all the way to the classroom. More than once Tomoyo had to stop her from going down the wrong walk way.

"Sakura, while I am happy for you, you should really focus a little more," said Tomoyo as they approached the classroom.

"What could be more important than my new-found love?" asked Sakura dreamily.

Sakura spent most of the day like that. Of course, she stopped daydreaming about the gorgeous boy with high cheekbones and well-kept hair. But her state of nirvana persisted, during which she cheerfully chatted with her friends at lunch, hummed her way through classes, and wore a grin as the math teacher called her up to solve a formula on the board. She got it wrong, but who cares?

Only one thing occurred to break her good mood during gymnastics practice. She had a significant spring in her step as she performed her backflips with no problem. Then came baton-twirling practice. Most often she could daydream and her hand's muscle-memory would expertly handle the twirling, throwing, and catching without a single input from her long-gone brain. But when she gazed across the field to the gate, and saw that amazing boy riding home on his bike with her brutish brother, Gary Wright's voice blasted through her mind once more. Her muscle-memory vanished, and down came the baton, right onto her head. Tomoyo prematurely finished her singing practice to take a sobbing Sakura home.

By the time the Kinomoto residence came into view, Sakura's pain-driven crying had reduced to a few sniffles and a whopping headache. They went inside, and a tremendous gust blew her sour mood away.

"Yukito!" cried the chestnut-haired girl.

"Hello again, Sakura," replied the charming boy. "Touya invited me over for dinner. Is that alright?"

"Of course it is!" exclaimed the girl. Sakura quickly remembered her manners and introduced Tomoyo. Her friend bowed, and shot the boy a mischievous smile.

"Oi! What happened to you?" said Touya, emerging from the bathroom. He checked the lump on Sakura's head and repeated his question.

"Sakura had an accident at training," said Tomoyo. "She's fine now."

"I'll be the judge of that," retorted Touya. He gripped her by her cheek and checked her eyes, before interrogating her with questions about her mental state, to which Sakura fired off well-practiced answers. She glanced at Yukito and murmured, "He does this every time I get hurt."

"Stop gettin' hurt then, Kaiju," said Touya.

A minute later, Touya stopped hopping on one foot while clutching the other in pain. Sakura glared at him cross-armed and repeated, "I am *not* a kaiju."

At that moment, the front door opened.

"Welcome back, Dad!" exclaimed Sakura.

When he entered the room, Mister Kinomoto greeted the new face in the room.

"Franklin Kinomoto," he said with a welcoming smile as he shook Yukito's hand.

"It is nice to meet you, Mister Kinomoto," replied Yukito. Both Sakura and Touya could sense he was surprised that their father was not Japanese. He did well to hide it though as he added, "Please call me Yukito."

"Well then, call me Franklin," said Franklin. "I hope you're going to stay for dinner. Who's on duty?" All eyes turned to the whiteboard on the wall. Sakura had kitchen duty. When Franklin turned to his daughter to announce her turn to cook, he noticed the lump on her head. He grew frantic, but was much more gentle than her brother had been. When he'd calmed down, he said, "It's alright. I can cook dinner tonight."

"I'll cook," returned the girl sternly. Tomoyo almost fell on the floor laughing.

Sakura cooked what she called *Karaage*[6] *à la Kinomoto*. All that really involved, though, was the addition of Chinese Five-Spice and rock salt to the breading before pan-frying, rather than deep-frying. It was her own special invention, which always made her happy. Add Yukito's presence to the aromas wafting from the pan, and she was straight back to humming 'Ren'ai Circulation'.

The chicken and accompanying salad was gone in twenty minutes flat.

---

6   Japanese-style fried chicken.

"I don't think anyone liked it, Sakura," said Franklin with a bewildered glance at the impeccably clean plates. "Would anyone like some tea?"

At that, Tomoyo stood from the table and said, "I should be going. I need to finish the sea creatures report for biology."

Sakura, who had heretofore been enthralled in everything Yukito had said, suddenly choked on her own sharp gasp.

"That's due day after tomorrow, isn't it?" she murmured.

Tomoyo's eyes widened. "You haven't started it yet, have you?"

Sakura gripped her head and moaned, "And I completely forgot everything from when we went to the aquarium!"

Franklin shook his head and sternly intoned, "Well, now you'll learn to take notes for next time."

"Dad, could you take me to the aquarium tomorrow afternoon?" Sakura pleaded, but Franklin declined.

"I've got late-night classes at the university tomorrow," he said.

"I've got one of my part-time jobs," said Touya when Sakura gazed at him longingly.

"Oh, come on, Big Brother! You've got part-time jobs everywhere. Couldn't you just call in sick for one of them?" exclaimed Sakura.

"Do my chores for a week and I'll think about it," retorted the boy. Sakura fumed. Sensing an impending argument, Tomoyo interjected, "I'll take you."

"No," interjected Franklin. "Miss Daidouji, you have *your* homework to do. Sakura will just have to face up to the consequences, and learn how to prioritise her studies over making videos."

Sakura withdrew into her chair with a gloomy look of resignation. The gods must have taken pity on her, because they made Yukito offer, "How about I take you tomorrow? I don't have any homework or part-time jobs. I can take you, if you want."

Sakura gazed at the boy, then to her father who nodded acquiescently. Her insides lit up with rainbows and a thousand-voice choir bellowing halleluiah. She sprinted around the table and gripped Yukito's hand.

"Thank you so much, Yukito!" she exclaimed as she jumped on the spot. "My saviour!"

"Run! The kaiju's gonna start a tsunami!" exclaimed Touya sardonically. He never saw the fist coming.

* * *

Kero cradled his big-eared head on his hands as he watched Sakura race about her bedroom. She pulled a cream-coloured one-piece dress with pink floral patterns over her head and checked herself in the mirror. This was the third dress she'd tried on, and to Kero it was just as fine as the other two.

"You know you're wastin' time you could be spendin' with this Yukito kid?" he murmured.

Sakura fumed, "I just want to make sure I look nice."

"This ain't a date, ya know," said Kero. "Ain't this cuz you got an assignment for school?"

"Who cares? It's Yukito!" exclaimed Sakura.

Her priorities're completely whack, thought the Beast of the Seal. He floated to her with a sigh, and zipped up the back of the dress.

"Sakura, this dress is fine," he said sternly. "Now get going or the aquarium will close."

Sakura glanced at him, and then turned to the mirror. Her brow knitted with frustration, and her inner voices still screamed, "Not good enough!" Eventually, Kero's more insistent voice broke through and she accepted her appearance. She sprinted to the entrance and donned her shoes.

"Don't steal any sweets," she said. "I won't be able to explain it away like with the chocolate puddings."

"Of course not, my Master," said Kero with a forced standard accent. Sakura noticed his hands behind his back, and she narrowed her eyes suspiciously.

"You'd better not be crossing your fingers behind your back," she grumbled.

"Get goin' already!" exclaimed Kero with a grin that Sakura returned as she shut the door and locked it behind her. Kero hung there in mid-air a moment longer, before his grin turned truly mischievous. He floated past the TV, foregoing Touya's games, and slid his way under the kitchen window. The guardian made his way down the footpath, eying Sakura as she hopped onto the bus.

"Tomoyo?" he called out, and the girl appeared out of the bushes with a collapsible scooter and an equally playful expression.

"Shall we?" murmured Tomoyo.

Kero hopped into the pocket of the girl's long yellow jacket, and they sped down the street on the scooter, staying just within eyesight of the bus. They didn't stay with it for long, as the bus had its own route to pick-up and deliver passengers beside Sakura. Instead, Tomoyo took another route, directly to the aquarium.

* * *

Sakura reached South Ikebukuro a little past four, and found the Sunshine Aquarium just in time to see Yukito standing at the front door. When his scanning eyes caught sight of her, he threw her a warm smile and hurried over to meet her.

"Sorry I'm late!" said Sakura. "I had to wait a little too long for the bus."

"That's alright, I grabbed tickets for us," said Yukito. Sakura beamed and followed him into the building. She was of course diligent in remembering why she was there, and pulled a notebook from her bag with a checklist of things she had to take notes on.

"I am gonna ace this assignment," she said with manic

resolve.

At first, she took lots of notes, especially on the huge orange fishes with human-like teeth, and the procedures for keeping the sea lions healthy. She'd already filled three pages worth of notes on starfish, crabs, zarigani[7], eels, and pelicans. To be fair, it had been Yukito who broke her rare bout of concentration when he said, "Hey, check it out! It's Dory!"

The yellow-tailed blue fish glanced at him as if it really was named 'Dory,' before it suddenly darted away and into the forest of coral. He chuckled and glanced in Sakura's direction. Predictably, everything else around her drained of meaning.

Oh, Utada Hikaru, you're so singing my bridal waltz, thought the entranced girl.

"How are you going with your notes?" asked Yukito.

"Oh, I've got a tonne," replied Sakura. She gave a yawn. "I'm a little hungry."

"Allow me to treat you, M'lady," said Yukito with a gallant bow that made Sakura giggle.

They left the tanks and found one of the aquarium's food halls. Sakura only had a small lunch box and an orange juice, so it was understandable when her jaw hit the ground at the sight of Yukito's meal.

"Hopefully this'll tide me over until dinner," he said. He winced when he saw Sakura's flabbergasted face. "I guess I'm a bit of a pig," he murmured. "I just can't move if I don't eat a lot."

"I was going to ask if you were a Hobbit," intoned Sakura. Then another thought occurred to her and she cried, "Oh no! I mustn't've served you enough last night."

"Oh, not at all! It was plenty, and delicious!" Yukito insisted. "I'll have to ask for Karaage à la Kinomoto again soon."

"Any time," replied Sakura as she hoed into her bento

---

7   Japanese species of crayfish.

box.

"Well, probably not unannounced," said Yukito. "I wouldn't want to bother your father, you see."

"Don't be silly," said Sakura with a dismissive wave of her hand. "Dad likes the rowdiness of a large group."

Yukito laughed at that, and said, "I wanted to ask about him … Your father, I mean." He started to stammer.

"He's not Japanese," said Sakura. "He's from Britain, and moved to Japan when he married Mum. He teaches history at Toudai."

"Ah, now it makes sense," said Yukito. "What did your mother do?"

"She was a model. She worked all over the place, and met my father while doing a show in London. Dad says it was love at first sight, and he dropped everything to come to Japan and marry her."

"Whoa! That sounds amazing," exclaimed Yukito. "He must've been completely head over heels." Sakura grinned proudly. Yukito went on, "Well, *my* father always told me I should wait for an invitation rather than show up unannounced. So I should make sure your father is alright with it."

Ah, such a gentleman, and totally not like my brute big brother, she thought.

"What do your parents do, if I may ask?" she said after finishing a mouthful of sushi.

"Ah, they passed away long ago," replied Yukito with a bittersweet smile. Sakura's insides turned to lead and she almost choked on her food.

Why did you ask that, you stupid, stupid, stupid!

"But it's alright," Yukito said quickly. "I lived with my grandparents up in Sendai, but I came here for my last few years of school. I hope to get into Toudai. Maybe if your father likes me, he can put in a good word."

In an effort to blast away her queasiness, Sakura blurted, "Of course, he will. And *I'll* put in a good word to him too!"

Yukito grinned, "I'll have to make sure I'm extra nice to you and Touya then."

Sakura held out her hand and said, "It's a deal, Mister Tsukishiro!"

The moment their hands touched, the hairs on the back of Sakura's neck stood on end. Her heart did a backflip as she sensed something.

A Clow Card!

A concerto of horrified gasps and screams filled the halls of the aquarium, all centred around one of the penguin pens. Sakura launched from her seat and charged toward the pen that was also the source of the Clow Card signature. The screech only she could hear emanated from a whirlpool that violently dragged one of the zookeepers under the water. Terror gripped Sakura even tighter when she saw who was struggling beneath the surface.

"Touya!" cried Yukito. Before Sakura could say a word, the boy had launched himself over the railing and into the pen. He managed to clear the penguin's swimming water in that single bound, and quickly scanned the pen for something to hold. He found an overhanging branch of a tree that was part of the pen, and gripped it as he held his hand out to Touya. Cheers from the crowd, the loudest being from Sakura, encouraged him as he caught his friend's hand and pulled with all his strength.

The invisible drowning force must have decided at that point to suddenly release its prey. Touya flew out of the water and onto dry land, coughing and spluttering, and scaring away a bunch of rather curious penguins. When he stood up alive, the whole crowd cheered.

Sakura wiped away her tears, and applauded her brother's saviour.

Oh, he's so unbelievably cool and sweet and strong!

Barely a few metres away, Tomoyo and Kero observed the action. Tomoyo sighed delightfully and said, "Sakura has picked the best boyfriend, hasn't she?"

Kero had a different expression as he eyed the water

below. He saw what Sakura was just learning to sense: the tiniest glimmer of light from a hull of translucent scales as it vanished into a pipe at the bottom of the pen. Then he turned to Yukito, and noticed something Sakura might never notice.

I wonder if he knows, thought the Beast of the Seal.

3 | Heist at the Aquarium

Sakura's eyes glazed over as the sun veered toward the horizon. For the whole day, her brain was locked on either Yukito or the Clow Card hiding in the aquarium. Even though the end of classes drew near, her mind showed no signs of letting go of either of those obsessions.

I only just managed to finish that assignment, she thought in between obsessing. She had Kero to thank for that, as he had diligently held her at her desk until she finished the report. Then, as they discussed what she'd seen at the aquarium, he had said something that was partly responsible for her immovable train of thought.

"You ain't got no chance," he'd said. "If what ya said is true, then that's the Watery Card. It's one of the master elemental Cards, meanin' it's too powerful for ya."

"There's gotta be a way," Sakura had insisted. "It almost drowned Touya. And it's not long before it'll kill someone."

"You figure out how to catch water in water, and we'll go," said Kero.

She hardly slept that night, and was a zombie the next day. Whenever she managed to fixate her mind on the Watery Card, it immediately missed its target and landed on Yukito saving her brother, and looking damn smashing doing it.

Tomoyo pursed her lips disapprovingly as she eyed her friend yawning her way through final period. She kept silent even as they walked home, watching Sakura trudge along, hunched over and drowsy.

"You should really make sure you get some sleep," said Tomoyo.

"When I Watery the catch Card," murmured Sakura.

Tomoyo shouldered her friend the rest of the way to her house, up to her bedroom, and laid her down. The girl was out like a light the moment her head hit the pillow. Kero floated above Tomoyo's shoulder, a tad perturbed by his master's state.

"She was fretting all day over the Watery Card, and didn't sleep last night," said Tomoyo.

"I told her she couldn't catch it," replied Kero. "Didn't think it'd bother her this much."

"Well it is, so what are you going to do?" asked Tomoyo sternly. "She's your master, right?"

Kero crossed his arms, his furry brow knitted with thought as he floated to the desk where the Book of Clow rested. He looked over his shoulder and mumbled, "We need to think. Don't worry about Sakura, we'll take care of her."

Tomoyo eyed her friend, out-cold on the bed. Then she bowed and left. When the door closed, Kero's eyes glimmered red, and the book wafted open to release the four Cards that called Sakura 'master.' They twirled about the Beast of the Seal, and their minds merged with his.

"It's been a long time since we spoke this way," said Windy with a stroke of her long blonde hair. Her straightforward gaze went around the circular table, and saw fifteen empty seats. The three other Cards lamented the vacancies, and the loneliness that crowded the once bustling room. Kero sat at the middle of the table, as the sun the Cards orbited. His red-glimmering eyes surveyed them.

"The Watery Card has revealed itself," he said. "At

present, our master's strength is not enough. How might we assist her in this goal?"

Fly finished stroking her feathers and glanced to Windy seated to her left.

"Neither of us have power against Watery," she muttered, her beak deforming like a human mouth around her words.

Windy smiled and added, "We have power, but of a different kind." She glanced over to Wood, partway between where Watery and Earth would sit. Wood did not share Windy's more vibrant demeanour, and remained pensive even as Windy said, "Perhaps if Wood and I were to collaborate?"

"Defeating him is not the solution," returned Wood with a slow, deliberate tone to her every syllable. "Watery is an aggressive Card as opposed to our more controlled, docile forms. We could hold him at bay for a short time, but not indefinitely. No, his true power comes in his shape-shifting ability. It is not defeat for which we should strive, but to deprive him of malleable form."

Kero pursed his lips, having instantly figured out a way to thwart the Card. But another thought occurred to him, and he reminded himself that he was not the Cardcaptor.

This is Sakura's duty, he thought. *I cannot capture the Cards for her. She must do it, in anticipation of the Final Judgement. She must pass this test herself.*

"I will pass this onto our master," he said aloud. "Let's hope she can discover the answer." When Fly, Windy, and Wood bowed, Kero turned to Jump. The humanoid rabbit's eyes aloofly wandered about the room, and a finger was stuck up its nose. He didn't remove the finger even when he noticed the others gazing at him.

"Oh, hey!" he blurted nasally. "When did you guys get here?"

Kero shook his head, his large ears twitching with annoyance as he said, "Never mind, Jump. Just keep doin' whatcha doin'." To the other Cards he said, "May we with honour serve the master of the Clow Cards."

The Cards bowed, before the room melted away and they returned to their inert forms within the book. Sakura was still asleep, using one of her stuffed toys as a cuddle pillow and sleep talking about manju[8]. Kero floated out of the room, and let his master sleep a while. Lucky for him, neither Touya nor Franklin were around, which meant he could look about the house all he liked. He drifted over to the TV, grabbed the gamepad, and booted up *Super Mario Maker*.

"You watch, RubberRoss, I'm gonna beat your levels!" he growled.

A torturous two hours later, Kero floated back into Sakura's bedroom, his eyes bloodshot from a combination of over-focus and frustrated rage. His continued failure to best those infuriating levels almost pushed his thoughts regarding Watery right out of his head. He plopped down on the bed next to Sakura, just as the girl started to wake.

"What's the matter?" asked Sakura upon noticing Kero's scowl.

"Curse you, RubberRoss," replied Kero. Sakura chuckled before yawning away the rest of her fatigue. She checked her clock and moaned, "Only six-thirty? I'm going to have so much trouble getting to sleep later on."

"Never mind that, Sakura," said Kero as he floated above the bed. "I talked over a few things with the Cards. If you wanna catch Watery, you'll need to catch it in physical form. Like, split it from the rest of the water."

"How would I do that?" asked Sakura with a dopey look. "I could grab a syringe and pump it out?"

Kero gave her a raised eyebrow and a smirk. He said, "You can't be serious. You'll be more likely to suck up the aquarium water instead."

Sakura's brow knitted with thought, but her mind was still a little weighed down by lack of sleep. She hopped off

---

8   A Japanese sweet, made of pastry filled with sweet bean paste.

her bed and trotted down stairs to the kitchen, where, in the pantry, awaited a perfectly nice bottle of pancake mix she'd bought with her allowance. Ten minutes later, the pair sat enjoying the sugary goodness. Kero wolfed his down before Sakura had even finished making her stack, and he was hankering for more. He didn't get a second helping, though, before the front door opened.

"I'm home," came Touya's voice. Kero sped across the table and plonked down lifeless on Sakura's shoulder, just as her brother entered the kitchen and noticed the extra plate on the table. "Who were you eating with, eh?" he asked suspiciously.

Sakura didn't notice Touya eying the teddy bear on her shoulder as she bluffed, "I just had seconds is all."

Touya's eyes narrowed a little. Then he said, "Whatever." He grabbed the used fork, reached across the table to Sakura's plate and pinched a slice.

"Hey! Those are *my* pancakes! I brought them with *my* allowance!" cried Sakura.

"Hmmm … Stolen pancakes," murmured Touya as he held his sister at bay with one hand while stealing more pancakes with the other. Sakura's onslaught promptly stopped with the sound of another voice.

"Pardon the intrusion," said Yukito as he appeared at the kitchen door. Sakura's eyes lit up with joy.

"Yukito!" she exclaimed.

"Are you making pancakes?" the boy asked innocently.

"Would you like some?" Sakura offered. "It can be thanks for helping me yesterday, *and* saving my brutish big brother."

"I'm sure Touya would like some too," said Yukito, which made Sakura cringe internally. She begrudgingly held her smile and said, "Of course. Sharing is caring!"

"I'm not hungry, thanks," said Touya with a yawn.

Sakura set to work on Yukito's pancakes, while listening in as best as she could to her brother's conversation. She heard the mention of the aquarium, and asked, "Oh, Touya. What about the accident yesterday? Do they know what happened?"

"Nope," replied Touya with an irritated edge to his voice. "Somebody else almost got done in by whatever it was. So the aquarium's gonna close until they can figure out what's wrong."

No, thought Sakura. *If they close the aquarium, Watery might escape and I won't be able to catch it. I've got to figure out a way.*

Sakura almost burnt the pancakes in her musings, but saved them quickly and served a four stack for Yukito.

"You sure you aren't going to have any?" Yukito asked Touya as he poured a generous coating of honey over the stack.

"Nah, there was plenty of syrup in those snow cones we had on the way home," replied Touya.

Snow cones!

It was as if Sakura's brain had been struck by lightning, and she grinned excitedly. She threw her arms around Touya and Yukito, and ecstatically screamed, "You two are the best! Thank you so much!" She then raced out of the kitchen and up to her bedroom.

"So, whadaya figure out?" moaned Kero as he recovered from Sakura's sudden burst of speed up the stairs.

"Ice," said Sakura with a grin. "That's how I can catch Watery. Freeze it!"

"How?" asked Kero, his sceptical look a perfect mask for his elation at his master's brain-blast.

Sakura sat down in front of her laptop, and called up a map of Tokyo. Before long she was looking at a squiggly blue line leading from the aquarium, southwest toward a building that made her grin triumphantly. She glanced at the Book of Clow and asked in a businesslike fashion, "Fly, you can travel a few kilometres, right?"

The Fly Card floated out of the book and its avian voice said, "No problem, my Master."

"Jump, you'll be her backup," said Sakura. The Jump

Card twirled in response. Then Sakura turned to the Wood and Windy Cards and said, "You'll be my leading gals. Let's catch Watery."

"Yes, Master," said the Cards, their caricatures smiling confidently.

* * *

Tomoyo stood out the front of a building just next to the Tozai Train Line, and shivered in the late-night cold. She giddily focused on her phone, which displayed a HUD bordering a live-feed of Sakura and Kero. She giggled at the sight of the blue jester costume she'd designed for her superhero friend.

I should design something a little more functional, though, she thought. As she eyed the balaclava over Sakura's mouth, she added, *Maybe a mask or helmet wouldn't be a bad idea.*

"Sakura, I'm in position at the rink," she said.

"Is it closed?" Sakura replied as she gazed at the camera.

"Yeah, but there are still a few people around," said Tomoyo.

"Great," said Sakura. "This drone you got is amazing. We can plan things across a whole city. You can tell your Mum her company's product works."

Tomoyo smiled at the prospect of pleasing her mother. Then her voice grew nervous as she said, "You sure this is a good idea?"

"It's a brilliant one," returned Sakura with a devious grin.

Kero floated next to her with arms crossed and a raised eyebrow. He said, "You're really proud of this idea, aren't you?"

"It's a stroke of genius!" Sakura exclaimed confidently. To the camera she said, "Tomoyo, you sure you can follow me with this drone?"

"Oh please, my Dear Sakura, I've been practicing ever since I saw you with the Fly Card," replied Tomoyo.

Sakura gazed up the wall she stood beside, huffed a few times to steel her resolve, and then took the Shadow Key from around her neck.

> *Key who conceals the Magic of Shadow,*
> *Ye who is more than ye seems:*
> *I command thee to bestow*
> *The power ye deems.*
> *Let us fulfil our vow*
> *In time's great streams … Release!*

The Shadow Key transformed into the Sealing Staff with a flash. Sakura struck it against the Jump Card, and wings formed on her ankles. Kero followed her up to the roof of the aquarium building, across which they dashed toward a padlocked access hatch. Sakura struck the Wood Card, and summoned a patch of roots to prise the lock apart. In less time that it took to order a coffee, they were inside the aquarium building.

The air-conditioning systems on the top-most floor roared, and Sakura had an epiphany. She held up the Windy Card.

"Go into the vents and find any security guards for me, okay?" she murmured, before striking the Card with the staff. Windy appeared in all her resplendence, and with a confident smile she flew into the air-conditioning vents. Sakura called out to her, "We'll go on ahead."

She, Kero, and Tomoyo's drone hopped through the fire-exit door, and down the spiral of stairs that led down into the building. Kero stopped her at the third floor door, where the penguin pens were.

"Windy says there's a couple of guards makin' their rounds," he whispered. He paused a moment, before his expression filled with alarm. "One's comin' from this door, the other's comin' from the floor below. Windy says they're heading upwards."

Sakura's breathing hitched and her heart raced. Her

gaze darted around as she tried to think quickly.

What do I do? I can't get arrested, or Dad'll freak, she thought.

"A distraction," whispered the drone. "There's a gift shop on the first floor with a bunch of stuffed animals."

A light switched on in Sakura's head and she whispered, "Kero! Draw the guards down there and —"

"Got it!" returned Kero, before promptly swooping down the stairs. Sakura launched herself up the stairs, using Jump to bounce off the concrete walls, until she passed the fourth floor door. The door started to open, and she swiftly flipped over the handrail and cowered on the stairs leading back to the fifth floor.

Bang!

Sakura winced, and her body trembled excitedly. She stifled her relieved gasp when she heard the guards exclaim, "Something down on the first floor. Let's go." The tapping of their feet on the stairs echoed up the concrete waveguide and pounded on Sakura's overly sensitive ears. She glanced down the shaft and saw the third-floor door clear. She dashed downward, trying to keep her steps light, and slipped through the door.

The aquarium looked a lot more foreboding at night, and that didn't help Sakura's nerves. The horror stories Touya told her as a child came to mind, and she almost bailed out of the whole thing.

"Sakura, are you all right?" murmured the drone.

"Just a little scary at night," Sakura whispered.

A soft flow of air billowed out of a ceiling duct and retook the shape of Windy. Her encouraging smile restored Sakura's confidence as she retook her inert form. Her voice flowed through Sakura's mind, "Kerberus distracted the guards, and he's hiding in the gift shop. Let's catch Watery."

"Right!" said Sakura.

She sprinted to the penguin pen, the residents of which had given their swimming water a wide berth. Sakura brandished her Sealing Staff.

"Watery! Come and get me!" she bellowed.

The surface of the water shuddered, and then exploded. A vicious beast formed within the liquid, and roared as it charged her. Sakura swiftly dashed back down the corridor toward the fire escape. Kero stood there waiting, and gasped at the sight of the torrent of living water. It growled fiercely as it edged nearer and nearer to Sakura's winged feet. It followed them up the staircase and out onto the roof, where it rose above the building and roared.

Sakura cast out a Card and cried, "Cage him in thy roots, Wood!"

A forest grew out of thin air to envelop the creature, which fought back against its vines and leaves.

"I shan't hold long," murmured Wood.

"Let me help her," said Windy in Sakura's mind.

"No, recover your strength, Windy," returned Sakura. To her feet she said, "Jump, let me know when you're tired."

"No probs, Ma'am," said Jump.

Sakura glared at the water beast and said, "Let's go!"

She jumped off the roof, her leap sending her across hundreds of metres in a single bound. Wood diligently held the flow of water in the air, and let it dash after the girl, who bounded off building walls in an effort to stay ahead of the torrent. Sakura knew that people would see the show – and thanks to the Internet, the whole world was soon to see it too. Luckily, she was disguised.

Jump started to tire, as evidenced by the shorter and shorter leaps Sakura could manage. Plus, her ankles were starting to hurt from the landings. She struck the Fly Card with her wand, and wings sprouted from her shoulders to carry her the rest of the way. Her destination came into view.

"Sakura, Wood's gettin' tired!" shouted Kero.

Sakura recalled the Card in mid-air, and sent out Windy

to catch the writhing water monster. She held her hand out to the beast, and searched out Windy's soul with her mind. When she felt the flow of Windy's essence girdling Watery's form, she willed the flow to branch out in tendrils about the water mass. Watery roared even louder, heralding its growing wrath.

I have to finish this!

Sakura swooped downward, dragging Watery and Windy with her mind. She hurled the mass through the vents in the building's roof, and Windy obeyed her mental commands. The wind sprite carried Watery's essence into the building's main chamber, far colder than the outside air, and hurled the beast against the icy floor of the skating rink. Sakura burst through the doors of the skating rink, with Tomoyo's drone in tow. Watery rose above the ice, and revealed its form: a majestic piscine humanoid, baring its fangs ferociously.

Sakura stood before it and grinned, "Gotcha!"

She raised her hand and pressed against the air before her. Windy mimicked her gesture, and made herself a wall against Watery's advance. Sakura began to twirl the Sealing Staff, directing Windy's flow like a conductor of a thousand-piece orchestra. The flow of air supercooled in contact with the ice, and drew all the heat from the water beast as it blew over it in frigid gusts and strokes. Watery growled and shrieked as it tried to pull away from it's frozen extremities, but struggling only drained its dwindling energy. By the time Windy was finished, Watery's face was a mask of defeat, with the slightest twinge of admiration for its soon-to-be master.

"Return to thine intended form, Clow Card!" Sakura bellowed as she struck the air before her. The ice sculpture before her eroded away in a shimmering gush of light, which left behind a Card bearing Watery's impressed effigy.

"You rock, Sakura!" shouted Kero gleefully.

Sakura picked the Card up, grinning triumphantly. She

looked to the drone that Tomoyo had managed to pilot all the way from the aquarium, and gave her winning pose. She couldn't hold it for long before she heard a chorus of shouts from the edge of the rink. Her heart froze as she saw a group of spooked security guards, brandishing guns and Tasers, demanding to know her identity.

Oh right, they don't recognise me, she thought. She summoned the Fly Card once more, soared past the baffled guards, and out the door. Kero followed close behind, the drone in his hand.

Tomoyo stood amid a crowd of amazed spectators, and with a smile watched her friend disappear into the night.

* * *

There was a building on the other side of the Tozai Line, on the roof of which stood a figure in the shadows. That figure gazed at the flabbergasted crowd, twinkling with the light of phone screens tweeting the event. He sneered angrily as he glared at the speck flying toward the horizon.

"The Clow Cards are not toys," he growled. "No way will *she* pass the Final Judgement." He gazed to the sky above and said, "Dear Ancestor, you have chosen your heir poorly."

4 | Tomoyo's Treasure

Sakura let out a hefty sigh and turned to Kero, who floated next to her in front of the green screen. He returned an overtly cocky grin that covered most of his plush-toy face.

"A New York accent?" she murmured in English.

"Why not? Fits with the Kansai," replied Kero. He struck a mid-air pose, "And New York is cool!"

Tomoyo could only pick up a few of their English words, but decided to leave them to their bickering as she checked the recording. She was careful to save the video file with the tag *English Version*, so as not to erase the Japanese version they'd previously recorded.

"Perfect," she chirped, drawing the attention of her actors. "I'll edit all this together and upload it later on."

Sakura hopped off the stool on which she'd perched for the last forty-five minutes, and stretched. Tomoyo closed down her computer and led her friends out of the studio that was her walk-in wardrobe. The maid entered the room, giving Kero just enough time to plop down on Sakura's shoulder, and make like a toy. In the middle of the large bedroom, she placed out a serving of tea and cake for the friends, before turning to Tomoyo.

"Young Miss, your mother will be arriving shortly," she announced.

"Thank you, Sayoko," replied Tomoyo. "Oh, by the

way, could you bring my mother's special box please?"

"At once, Young Miss," said the maid, closing the door behind her. The clack of the lock brought Kero back to life.

"This's gettin' real annoyin', ya know," he mumbled. His mood quickly changed as Tomoyo set out a cup of tea and a slice of cake. Thereafter, the only sound he made was that of satisfied sighs.

Sakura, conversely, was content to let her eyes wander about her best friend's bedroom. Though she'd been there plenty of times for measuring, costume fittings, and shooting scenes for her videos, her friend's lifestyle never ceased to amaze her. Tomoyo's voice brought her attention back to the table.

"I'm glad we were able to make those recordings," said Tomoyo.

Sakura frowned sceptically, "Yeah, I'm still not sure a disclaimer is going to convince people these videos aren't real."

"Pah! It's a chance to expand my Internet following," exclaimed Kero with a mouthful of tea-soaked cake. "The world must see more of my coolness!"

"Even though they think you're a CGI character?" retorted Sakura. Kero shot her the evil eye, before promptly shoving his cake down his gullet.

"It's just a precaution after the news linked the Watery incident to our channel," said Tomoyo. "I'm not too worried though, since even the people on the news started to doubt the official reports because they were so similar to our videos."

"See! I told ya a video channel was a good front," exclaimed Kero, his spoon stabbing the air above him in a triumphant pose.

Sakura and Tomoyo just shot him a blank stare, and in a unified chorus they murmured, "Weren't you the one opposed to the idea?"

Kero evidently wasn't listening as he further

proclaimed, "We should also do a Kerberus' Corner, where I talk about all Sakura's costumes!"

Tomoyo's unity with Sakura suddenly broke, and she clapped her hands together, "Oh, what a good idea!"

"And a Let's Play, too!" added Kero.

Sakura sank back into her usual mode of letting the pair plot and scheme.

I guess I'm just along for the ride, she thought, though she could not help but feel excited about their various schemes.

The door thudded as someone tapped a knuckle against it. Kero leapt onto Sakura's shoulder in time for Tomoyo to answer the door. In bounded a woman with Tomoyo's eyes and hair, if the latter was only slightly shorter. Her white suit jacket was handed to the maid as she embraced her daughter. When the woman laid eyes on Sakura, she exploded into a paroxysm of joyous ramblings.

"You're Sakura! Oh, how wonderful it is to meet you! You're such a darling! Ooooh, I could just hug you and squeeze you and love you to pieces!"

And boy didn't she.

Bearing the sudden onslaught of hugs, Sakura winced as Kero fell off her shoulder and landed on his head. Commendably, he managed to keep quiet.

"Oh, where are my manners?" said the woman as she slowly sobered. "I'm Tomoyo's mother. Please call me Sonomi."

"Nice to meet you, Sonomi," said Sakura in between startled pants. She grabbed Kero from the floor and returned him gently to her shoulder. Sonomi eyed the plush toy, and Sakura introduced him.

"Ah! This is the Cardcaptor's side-kick," said Sonomi. "I love your videos. You and my daughter make such an amazing team."

Sakura giggled bashfully. Sonomi turned to Tomoyo, brandished a USB drive, and said, "Speaking of which ..."

Tomoyo's eyes lit up in a manner that Sakura only saw

when she was plotting something amazing.

"Finally the sound engineers finished!" she exclaimed. She took the drive and plugged it into the large TV across the room from her bed. Her mother bounced on her toes like a two-year-old as Tomoyo navigated to the video file and hit play. At first, the screen was blank, then a cherry blossom petal wafted down from the top of the screen, and hit a heretofore-unseen liquid surface. When it hit, a sweet tune started playing, and Sakura recognised the song instantly.

Blood drained from her face when she saw a flurry of shots of herself in Tomoyo's hand-made red frilly costume. Then came the logo, *'Cardcaptor Sakura.'* As the anime-style music video played, Sakura edged to her twinkly-eyed friend and muttered, "What the heck is this?"

"It's the opening for our show," replied Tomoyo in a dreamy voice.

"Oh, she's so cute," moaned Sonomi.

"That's my voice singing," mumbled Sakura.

"Hm-hm! I recorded you the last time we were at karaoke," replied Tomoyo. Sakura's insides writhed with embarrassment, and she face-palmed.

The video finished with Sakura running down the street to meet with Tomoyo, laughing and talking their way toward the horizon. Then fadeout.

"This is going to be the first video on the channel!" Tomoyo announced. "Soon, record labels will demand to hear the heavenly voice of Dear Sakura."

"Don't forget Kerberus," shouted Kero.

Sakura froze, but Sonomi hardly noticed the tiny movement of the teddy bear on her shoulder and said, "Wow! You're really good at ventriloquy, Sakura."

"Sakura does the voice of Kero," said Tomoyo, eying the teddy bear with a sly grin. The Beast of the Seal's lips waged war with themselves to not upturn their corners.

The maid returned with a well-kept antique chest in her hands. She drew the attention of her mistresses with a polite clear of her throat. At Tomoyo's direction, the maid set the box beside the empty teacups and cake plates, which she then bussed as she exited the room.

"I wanted to show Sakura our treasure chest," said Tomoyo.

"But it won't open, Tomoyo," said Sonomi. "The lock mechanism is broken, and we need to get it repaired."

Sakura felt a tingle behind her ears as she eyed the chest.

I have felt this before, she thought.

"Here, Sakura, watch this," said Sonomi as she brandished a key. She inserted it into the lock, but it wouldn't turn. Moreover, the moment she let go of the key, it flew out of the slot and landed on the floor. Sakura recognised the signature. She glanced at Tomoyo, who raised her eyebrows as she mimed, "A Clow Card?"

"Definitely," she mimed in reply.

Sonomi moaned with disappointment, "It's really a bother, since I've got something that belongs to my dear sister in here."

"That's a shame," replied Sakura with the appropriate tone, but her face was blank as she stared at the box. Before she could mime to Tomoyo to get her mother out of the room, the maid returned and announced, "Missus Daidouji, Mister Namikawa of Yotsuba Bank is on the telephone."

Sonomi glanced down at the box one last time, gave a resigned sigh, and left the room to take her call. Tomoyo slyly closed the door behind her. Before she turned around, she heard Sakura softly whisper, "Release!"

The Sealing Staff materialised in her hands as Kero landed beside the chest, eying it suspiciously.

"I figure this is this Shield Card," he said.

Sakura gingerly edged the bird-head of her staff toward the box. The staff was suddenly thrown back, and Tomoyo shrieked with surprise.

"Yep, this is definitely Shield," said Kero.

Sakura gazed at the chest, her lips pursed as she wondered how she would seal it. Kero floated into the air above it, tapping his toes against the invisible barrier.

"How do I get it to reveal its true form?" asked Sakura.

"It'll only do that once it's finished guarding what it's … well, ya know, *guarding*," replied Kero.

"But why would it take our treasure box?" asked Tomoyo, her eyes riddled with worry for her prised possessions.

"It's drawn to really precious things," said Kero. "Though it doesn't really have manners and just does whatever it wants, it really is a nice Card. It's not psycho, like Watery, that's for sure."

"Well, should I just knock it in with one of the Cards I've got?" asked Sakura. She glanced around the room and added, "I'll try to be careful not to break anything."

"No good, girl," said Kero with a dismissive wave of his hand. "You might be able to break it if you had Sword, but ya don't."

"Well then, what should I do?" exclaimed Sakura.

While the pair bickered, Tomoyo chewed her finger thoughtfully. She glanced at Sakura, then Kero, and then the Cards in her friend's backpack. She remembered all the times Sakura had talked to the Clow Cards, which only she could hear. Tomoyo's eyes fell on the chest, and the key in her hand.

I guess it's worth a shot, she thought with a shrug. She waltzed over and knelt down in front of the chest. With a smile, she said, "Hello, my name's Tomoyo Daidouji." Sakura and Kero fell silent. Tomoyo continued, "Thank you for looking after my precious treasures, Mister Shield. I have the key here. Would you kindly let me open the box? If you'd please?"

There was a moment of silence, in which the three exchanged glances. Then the box started to glow, and a winged shield materialised from the light that wafted from it. The shield hovered above the chest, and bowed to

Tomoyo politely.

"Thank you very much, Mister Shield," she said before inserting the key and turning it. The chest popped open with a click. Tomoyo glanced at Sakura, who uttered her sealing incantation. The shield dissolved into its Card form and wafted into its new master's hand. Kero could only stare dumbstruck at what just happened.

"Tomoyo, that was brilliant," he said with a deadpan tone. "I knew Shield was nice, but not *that* nice."

"I thought he'd respond if I just asked," Tomoyo said, trying to hide her shyness. She glanced to Sakura, who wore a warm smile. "Sorry for upstaging Cardcaptor Sakura," she said sheepishly.

Sakura shook her head and said, "I've got half a mind to give this one to you."

"I don't have any magic," replied Tomoyo with a laugh. "I'm happy just to document your adventures ... Oh no! I didn't tape this one!"

Sonomi suddenly barged into the room with a huff, scaring the three occupants half to death.

"I can't believe that rat, Reiji," she growled before proceeding to mumble a string of insults at the banker on the telephone. Her sour mood was blown away when she saw the chest open. "You fixed it!" she cried with delight. "What was wrong with it?"

"Oh, Sakura found a spring in the lock was pushing the key back out," said Tomoyo with a wink her friend's way.

Sonomi threw her arms around Sakura and wiped away a tear. "Thank you so much, Sakura! You're amazing, aren't you? Handy with locks, and creative too. Just look at your Cardcaptor prop!"

Sakura's breath caught in her throat as she noticed the still active Sealing Staff in her hand.

"Oh yeah! We were just fiddling with the prop," she stammered. Her eyes fell to the chest. Within lay a preserved corsage that Sonomi delicately lifted out.

"This belonged to my dear sister," she explained. "She

passed away a long time ago, and I preserved these flowers for her."

Sakura grinned at the woman's bittersweet expression and said, "I'm sure she's very happy you're protecting that memory."

Sonomi sniffed away her tears, placed the corsage back in the box, and then excitedly grabbed Sakura's hand.

"I'm cooking dinner tonight!" she announced. She promptly dragged a bewildered Sakura out of the room, asking her what kinds of food she liked. Kero fell off her shoulder, partly on purpose, and when the mother was out of sight, he floated back over to Tomoyo. He gazed over her shoulder to see the felt sachet resting on the velvet padding of the box.

"That your special treasure?" he asked. "What's in it?"

"An eraser Sakura gave me when we first met," Tomoyo intoned with a smile.

Kero eyed the girl's warm expression with a grin. He gazed over his shoulder to the door, from where Sonomi's excited voice trickled, and asked, "If your mom's a good cook, you'd better save me some food."

Tomoyo beamed and bumped fists with the floating teddy bear, "You betcha!"

* * *

"*Dopyuu!*" murmured the figure that hid in the trees. Her sinister reptilian eyes narrowed as if zoning in upon the two girls having a meal with the older woman. She licked her lips with a sticky purple tongue, and glanced at the serpent staff in her hand.

"My mar-th-ter, the repwica you prepared doez indeed theaw the Cardz, *dopyuu!*" she murmured. In her other hand, she raised a Card with a bizarre repeating pattern emblazoned above the word '*The Illusion.*'

With a toothy grin, the being uttered, "*Fu-gu-gu-guuu!* I'w thoon test their yuth in combat."

5 | Ghost

For once Sakura woke up early. She actually felt quite rested, possibly on account of the dream that still lingered in the vortex of her waking mind: her mother, pushing her on a swing.

Must've been when I was four or something, she thought as she threw on her school uniform and brushed her hair. She stole a glance at Kero, still out like a light in the desk drawer she'd made into a bedroom for him.

"Gotta get past them thwomps," he mumbled, his tiny fingers twitching as if pressing buttons on a game controller.

Sakura grinned and left a note for him before heading to school. Franklin was on a trip to a dig, and Touya had an interview for college, so she only had to make breakfast for herself. She wolfed down a few slices of toast, and then she was out the door.

She was able to take a little longer on her commute to enjoy the scenery. The weather was starting to warm up, and she chuckled in anticipation of pool and beach. She skated a few blocks along, passing by the place where Touya usually met up with Yukito. But since she was out the door early, he wasn't there yet. She giggled giddily as an idea crept into her head. She detoured to the left, down the path Yukito took to reach the meet-up point, and found the name sign 'Tsukishiro' on the front gate of a traditional Japanese mansion.

It wasn't the first time she'd seen his house, but it was still quite the surprise every time she beheld it. Sakura could see the sliding doors opened into the garden, but no Yukito. She skated around to scan the yard, but the boy was nowhere in sight.

"Good Morning, Sakura," came that sultry voice. Sakura almost jumped three feet in the air as Yukito appeared from below a hedge bush. "You're out early," he added with a smile.

"Good morning, Yukito," Sakura stammered. "I got up early today. Just one of those days, I guess." She eyed the water can in his hands. "Were you gardening?"

"Yep, it's one of the conditions I have for staying here," said Yukito. "I keep the house perfectly in order for my Grandparents, and they let me live in their investment property for free."

"Lucky you," said Sakura. "I don't think my Dad has anything like this set up for Touya or me."

"Never mind that," said Yukito. "By the time you even think about that, you'll have married some great guy and be picking out your own house." The mention of marriage made Sakura flustered. Yukito checked his watch and said, "I'd invite you in for tea, but we'll both be needing to get to school soon. Would you like to come around after school?"

Sakura's heart fluttered, "That'd be wonderful!"

She promptly made a note in her mental day planner before bidding her friend farewell and continuing along on her commute. She sighed excitedly, and said to the sky, "Thanks, Mum, for waking me up early this morning!"

It was very strange sight to see the school before the alarm bell had gone off. Students were only just starting to reach the school, and Sakura managed to beat the bulk of the crowd by a few minutes. She was at her desk, daydreaming about chatting with Yukito over a cup of oolong, when Tomoyo plonked down at the desk in front of her with a surprised expression. They proceeded to chat about Sakura's rare early morning, before going on to discuss her imminent tea date. Naoko soon joined them to ask about their plans for their next Cardcaptor video (and whether she could star in it as Sakura's side-kick). Takeshi and Chiharu appeared soon after, and both had a perturbed expression.

"What's the matter, you two?" asked Tomoyo.

"We just passed the bridge near the preschool playground," said Takeshi. "We looked over the water and saw a ghost!"

Sakura scoffed, "Yeah, yeah, Takeshi. I'm not gonna get fooled today."

"He's not making it up," said Chiharu with a deadpanned voice. "It was a ghost! A real one! It jumped right out of the water and screeched at us."

Sakura's heart skipped beats and she fake laughed, "Oh, yeah, now Chiharu is starting to get into his rambles. Good one, you two." Her effort to stay casual was not remotely convincing.

Takeshi clutched his chest, genuine fear in his eyes, "This isn't a joke, Sakura. It's real."

Naoko was excited and said, "Really? What did it look like?"

Takeshi trembled as he recounted, "It had eight eyes, and a great big mouth full of fangs, and purple botchy skin."

A frustrated Chiharu moaned, "Oh, come on, Takeshi! Be serious for once!"

"But that's exactly what I saw!" the pale boy insisted.

"Well, *I* saw Sadako, with her long black hair all over her face," said Chiharu. "I thought she was going to consume my soul."

Sakura broke down as her mind involuntarily visualised the creature in her head. It made her shake uncontrollably and repeatedly make the sign of the cross over her chest.

"Did anyone else see it?" asked Tomoyo, a tad intrigued.

"We asked around, but no one else was on the bridge at the time," said Takeshi.

"And you both saw different things," Tomoyo concluded.

Takeshi and Chiharu grabbed Sakura's hands and pleaded, "Sakura, you have to use your magical powers to help us!"

Sakura stared right back at them, "I don't have magical powers."

"Oh, if only you did," exclaimed Takeshi. "You could bust that ghost!"

Tomoyo placed a hand on the pair's shoulders and said, "Now, now! We don't know what you saw. Like you said, you both saw different things. Maybe you'd just been daydreaming."

Sakura piped up, "Yeah, no way you saw a ghost, right? Ha ha! Just daydreaming!"

Tomoyo suddenly thrust her finger into the air and proclaimed, "We'll have to investigate after school!"

Sakura screeched with dismay. For the whole of morning and midday classes, she was a wreck. Whenever she had the chance, she tried to convince Tomoyo out of her decision to go and check the bridge. But when she did, Tomoyo only replied with, "It may be a you-know-what." That, unfortunately, did nothing to ease poor Sakura's nerves.

Math was the last period before lunch. Sakura tried to focus on the equations the teacher had put up on the board, but it was hardly her best subject. Clow Cards and reverse gainers, she could do. Find the determinant of a quadratic polynomial, no chance – especially when trying to keep her mind off ghosts.

Or aliens, her mind involuntarily murmured. The thought instantly elicited very unwanted images of the ugly monster from those old American space movies her brother made her watch as a child. Her whole body shuddered and she knocked her pencil case off her desk. The teacher waited while she tidied herself up, but she wasn't beyond chiding the girl.

"Miss Kinomoto, you should really pay more attention," said the teacher.

"Yes, Sensei," replied Sakura with a shaky voice.

The teacher rolled her eyes and returned to the board. She continued to write more formulae. She wrote all the way to the edge of the board, and continued onward. She kept on writing and writing, moving along the walls as her math devolved into squiggles and streaks. The students were at first amused, then confused, then very concerned. The marker hit the floor, and the teacher started to twitch and shudder. Then she swivelled to face the class, her eyes wide with murderous bloodthirst and tremendous horror.

"See? What! Do I!" she screeched. She crumpled to a heap on the floor, and tried very hard to push herself into the solid concrete wall as if to escape an invisible wight that possessed her.

Takeshi, who wasn't overcome by confusion and horror, knelt down to try and snap the teacher out of her hysteria. The moment he touched the teacher's shoulder, he gasped in fright, "The eight-eyed ghost has come back!" He grabbed Naoko, who was nearest to him, in horror and shouted, "Can't you see it?" Naoko was far less scared and more confused at what she suddenly saw.

"It's a porpoise!" she exclaimed.

Sakura, overcome by unwanted visions of horror movies, cowered behind Tomoyo who watched the event unfold with intrigue. A few teachers and students in the nearby classrooms came to investigate, and when they touched a student they were suddenly infected with this strange hallucination.

"But they're all seeing different things," Tomoyo thought aloud.

She advanced toward Naoko, who laughed at the sight

of a tap-dancing porpoise, and grabbed her shoulder. Then she turned to the teacher. She was still the same as she had been, cowered on the floor, gripping her hair, and begging the monster to leave her alone. Tomoyo scanned the room, and at first saw nothing out of the ordinary, until her eyes drifted to the window and saw something that confused her even more.

A pork bun?

A giant pork bun floated next to the third storey window of the school. Everyone else seemed to scream or laugh when they saw it.

"They *are* seeing different things," said Tomoyo.

Out the corner of her eye, she saw Sakura, still clung to her shirt. She too was looking out the window, but her expression was neither one of confusion or fear, but of joy.

"Mum?" she murmured. She released her friend, bolted to the window, and threw it open, and cried, "Mum! It's you, isn't it?" Elated and overjoyed, she climbed onto the nearest chair and leaped out of the window.

Tomoyo let out a horrified scream.

* * *

Sakura woke on a strange bed, in a different house: an old house that smelled of experience. She looked up at a grid of hardwood beams, supported by pillars lining each corner of the room. Her eyes drifted around, noting the fading daylight through the window. A door creaked open, and Yukito entered.

Sakura shot upright and opened her mouth, but only a mishmash of stammers and blabber came out.

"Have a good sleep?" asked Yukito, though there was a dash of concern to his normally cheerful manner.

"What happened?" Sakura managed to ask.

"You don't remember?" said Yukito as he handed her a mug of tea. "It seems there was a gas leak at your school. It made everyone see things. According to Miss Daidouji, you saw something that made you leap out of the window."

Sakura gasped, and quickly threw off the covers of the futon on which she'd been laying. Her legs were still there, and without bandages.

"Did someone catch me?" she asked.

Yukito cocked his head, and with a frown he said, "Yes and no." Sakura shot him an even more confused look, and he went on, "I had a free period and was a little hungry, so I was on my way to the shops. I heard the commotion, and then I saw you at the window. I almost fainted when I saw you jump, but I sprinted to catch you."

Sakura beamed, "My hero!"

"Ah, but it was weird," said Yukito. "As I was running, it was as if the wind had blown to cushion your fall."

"Was it Windy?" Sakura thought aloud.

"It was fairly windy, yeah," said Yukito. "But it seems someone up there really likes you, since they gave me time to catch you."

Sakura smiled, and sipped the tea. Her nerves relaxed a little more, and she found the mind to ask, "This must be our tea date, then?"

"I guess," said Yukito. "The school was closed for the rest of the day, and since Touya and Franklin weren't at home yet, I decided to bring you here. Miss Daidouji brought some pyjamas for you … Oh, don't worry. She changed you out of your uniform." He adjusted his glasses and added with an intrigued smile, "That girl must have some serious connections, considering the secret agents that came to pick her up."

"Oh, those would be her bodyguards," said Sakura. "Her mother runs Daidouji Incorporated."

Yukito's eyes widened, "She's *that* Daidouji? Wow! So those drones they're selling, you use them for your movies?"

"Something like that, yeah," said Sakura. She quickly dodged the subject of her videos, and moved onto the subject of school. "So, did they find the gas leak?"

"As far as I know," said Yukito. "No one else has been affected. Though I heard from Miss Daidouji that your teacher was quite upset about it. It was all on the news too."

An image of Kero tearing his fur out in front of the TV entered Sakura's mind, and she grew nervous.

I hope Kero doesn't get angry at me, she thought. Her apprehension must have leaked out onto her face, because Yukito soon after took the mug from her hand.

"You should have a bit more rest," he said calmly. "Touya said he'll be around in a little while longer."

Part of her mind groaned at the imminent teasing her brother would unleash upon her, but the rest of it was slowly infiltrated by fatigue. She laid back down, and let her mind clear. As she drifted off to sleep, she mumbled, "Yukito, I saw my mother at school. She was floating out the window. Do you think it was her ghost?"

Yukito smiled, "I don't think so."

"What if it was? What if she wanted me to do something?" she droned as sleep finally took her.

"Trust me, Sakura," said Yukito as he stroked her hair. "No mother would put her daughter in danger like that."

* * *

Sakura woke the next morning in her own bed. A note lay on her bedside table, written in her brother's handwriting: "Hey Kaiju, There's some bacon and eggs in the warming draw. Dad should be back some time during the day. Don't be rampaging around while school's out. Touya."

Sakura's eyes narrowed and she growled, "I'm not a kaiju!"

As if her voice was an alarm clock, Kero shot up from where he'd been sleeping on the bed, and looked over with bleary eyes. When he saw her, his face scrunched up and he shot through the air, his eyes fountains as he hugged Sakura's face.

"Sakura! I'm so sorry!" he screamed. "I almost lost my master! I'm a failure as a guardian!"

Sakura almost suffocated from his smothering hugs, and she prised him away from her face. She tried to calm the distraught teddy bear, but had to resort to a stiff flick to his head to snap him out it. He rubbed his head and said, "But, you almost got hurt! I shoulda been there to catch you!"

"Kero, it wasn't your fault," said Sakura. "It was a gas leak at school. Nobody could have prevented it. I was just lucky that I cast Windy at the time I did."

Kero frowned, "How do ya figure that? Did ya get the wand out and use it? Better not've been in front of everyone else."

Sakura thought back to her fall, and tried to remember what had happened. Eventually, she came up empty and shrugged, "Yukito told me that I floated down. I must've summoned Windy."

Kero's expression grew even more perturbed. At his mental command, the Book of Clow floated out of her desk draw and hovered over to her.

"How could ya have summoned Windy when she's been here the whole time?" he murmured.

Sakura drew a complete blank, and could not come up with any answer. Her head hurt, and she was still too tired, and scared, to think about that harrowing experience. She threw her hands up and said, "I dunno!"

That only annoyed Kero, and he shook his head irately as Sakura threw on her clothes with a carefree hum and went down for breakfast. Tomoyo showed up not long after breakfast. She was just as upset as Kero over Sakura's accident, and squeezed her to the point of strangulation. Just like Kero, she needed a good flick to the head to make her calm down. When everyone was settled and had a cup of tea in front of them, Tomoyo brought up the subject of the hallucinations.

"I don't think it was gas," she said curtly. "In fact, it

may be a Clow Card."

"But Tomoyo, ya ain't got no magic, so how could ya sense it?" asked Kero.

"I didn't, but it makes sense with what I saw," said Tomoyo. She turned to Sakura, "You saw your mother out the window."

"Yes, and she looked really sad, but at the same time happy to see me," said Sakura, her gaze growing distant and unfocused. "She called my name, and held her hands out to me. I was so happy to see her, I guess I forgot where I was."

"Do you know what *I* saw?" asked Tomoyo. "I saw a pork bun." Sakura and Kero's jaws hit the table. Tomoyo didn't wait for their comments and continued, "Naoko saw dancing animals, Takeshi saw the ghost from the bridge, and Sensei said she saw the worst kind of mess and disorder."

Kero's ears twitched, "Was it the teacher who started seein' things first?" Tomoyo nodded, and Kero snapped his fingers, "Ya might be onto somethin', Tomoyo. It was math class, right? The worst thing math teachers hate is messiness and disorder. That ain't changed in centuries. Euler was the worst, I'll tell ya. But then once the teacher started freakin' out, people got scared, I'm sure. So Fibber Boy goes 'n' touches her, and some effect got passed on, which materialises what's goin' on in their heads at the time. Fibber Boy sees somethin' scary. Naoko, who's into that kind of stuff, sees somethin' funny. Plus, it's, like, right before lunch so Tomoyo –"

"I was hungry," the girl interjected.

"And I'd had a dream about Mum," Sakura murmured. "But are you sure? If it really was Mum, then maybe she wants my help."

"To be honest, Sakura, I'd really like it more if it was ya mom," said Kero. "'Cuz, if this is a Clow Card, then it's the Illusion Card, and it's been thrown down in attack mode."

"Attack mode?" Sakura repeated.

Tomoyo giggled, "You've been watching *Yu-Gi-Oh*, haven't you?"

Kero grinned, but resisted the urge to rabble about anime. He floated above the table and looked at Sakura fixedly.

"From what I remember, when Illusion is left on its own, it don't work like how ya described it," he said slowly. "It usually just picks up a spot to camp and stays there. It *can* be used to infect people with madness, but only when commanded to."

Tomoyo gasped as Sakura caught Kero's meaning.

"Someone is controlling it?" she asked. "Another Cardcaptor?"

"Clow *did* have a lot of enemies," said Kero. "Loads of nutjobs wanted to copy his magic, and some even tried to make Sealin' Staffs to steal his Cards. I was worried that Sakura might have a problem with some idiot tryin' to swoop in. If that's it, they've nabbed Illusion, and maybe more. And they're tryin' to kill off the competition."

Sakura gripped the Shadow Key hanging from her neck. She shivered at the idea of the Clow Cards, dangerous on their own, being wielded as weapons against her. Kero kept his eyes fixed on her as he ruminated some more. Then he grabbed his tea and downed it, before shrugging, "Or Illusion's just bored."

The girls' faces almost went through their palms.

"Well, which one is it?" exclaimed Sakura irately. "If there's another Cardcaptor, will I still be able to seal the Illusion Card?"

"Shouldn't be a problem," said Kero as he refilled his cup. "Unless it's Clow himself, no fake'll up you. The Clow Cards'll always obey the holder of the Shadow Key before anyone else."

"And what if it's really my Mum?" Sakura asked.

Kero downed his tea, and gazed upward as he pondered. Then, with careful choice of words, he intoned,

"Ghosts *are* real … *real-ish*. And if it's ya mom, then I s'pose ya get to talk to her."

* * *

Moonlight irradiated the deserted school and adjacent streets. No one wanted to be near the building with a great big 'danger' sign over it. That made it all the more easier for those who knew better.

Sakura glanced downward at the yellow dress that was Tomoyo's latest costume. She'd described it as a functional suit, and although it had metal-reinforced shoulder pads and a helmet, the lower half was an umbrella-shaped dress with frills.

I guess Tomoyo really can't help herself, thought Sakura as she looked down with dismay. She touched her fingers to the helmet, which was not so much a helmet as it was a stylish set of noise-cancelling headphones. At least they were functional, with a wireless link to Tomoyo's phone.

The school gate was padlocked, but that was hardly anything for a magic girl. Sakura cast out the Jump Card, and carried Tomoyo over the fence, with Kero in tow. First, they went up to their classroom, and waited a moment for the hallucination to reveal itself. Then they looked through the rest of the classrooms on their floor, before heading out to the sports yard.

Sakura grew nervous and started to twirl her staff to relieve her apprehension. It didn't help that the air grew colder as the hour grew later, and there was still no sign of the spectre.

"If I'm not careful, none of us will get any sleep tonight," she droned.

Kero hunched and yawned, "Well, Illusion mightn't be here after all. We should prob'ly wait 'til he shows up."

"And if somebody else gets badly hurt?" Tomoyo intoned. Although she too considered calling it a night, as she noted the dwindling battery indicator on her camera. Her attention went back to Sakura, whose expression had changed. Tomoyo panned the camera to record what her friend was looking at. Initially, she thought it was moonlight reflecting off the surface of the pool. Then she looked away from her camera screen and used her own eyes.

The ball of light flitted above the pool, like a giant firefly. The girls looked to Kero, who shrugged obliviously. Sakura moved toward the pool gate, the Sealing Staff at the ready. The ball darted to the left, then to the right, before it finally found a comfortable spot in the air, and suddenly grew in size. It grew arms, legs, and a head, before cloaking itself in a pretty white dress.

Tomoyo's jaw dropped and she said, "That's not a pork bun."

"It's a lady," said Kero.

"Mum!" screamed Sakura. The Fly Card activated without a word from the master, and Sakura flew toward the pool. She hovered near the water's edge and confronted the serenely smiling woman with flowing hair. "Mum! It's you, isn't it?"

The lady smiled, and held her hands out. Though she made a welcoming gesture, she started to back away. Sakura started to panic, and swooped closer to the apparition, screaming, "Wait for me! Mum! Don't leave!"

She caught up to the ghost and threw her arms around the woman's neck. The lady smiled, and embraced her warmly. Then she suddenly dropped into the pool, taking Sakura with her. Kero launched himself over the wall in a fit of horror, but was thrown back by an immensely powerful barrier.

"What the heck?" he screeched. "Illusion don't have no power like that!" He threw himself at the barrier again, and was repelled even harder. "That ain't even Clow magic," he growled.

The pool was a flurry of splashing and waves, as Sakura struggled at the bottom of the deepest part. She opened her eyes, the chlorine stinging as she gazed up into the face of her mother's ghost. Still she serenely smiled as she held the girl down.

Why, Mum? Why are you hurting me?

Her lungs burned, but her struggling subsided as the woman's glad expression drained her muscles.

Are you lonely in Heaven? Do you want me with you?

Her eyes closed, and her arms fell limp. Her mind became dull fugue of emotion and memory, slowly emptying of any thoughts or cares. What seemed like her last thought crept up on her, like a friend saying bye as she went home from school.

It was Yukito's voice: "No mother would put her daughter in danger like that."

Tomoyo didn't have a chance to cry before a blast frightened her terribly. The barrier burst from within as the pool's water flew into the air and fell as rain. What remained heaved like the ocean during a typhoon, and hovering in the eye of that storm, Tomoyo and Kero saw the coolest thing ever: Sakura, her resplendent wings spread in all her sheer epicness, as Watery's form girdled her in a protective bubble.

"You are not my mother!" she roared, letting her friend's see her angry for the first time. The imposter gave a confused sneer as Sakura pointed the Sealing Staff at it and shouted, "As Master of the Clow, I command thee! Reveal thy true form!"

At that, the being's female form melted and twisted out of shape. Fractal spirals emerged from within the entity's being, and billowed all the colours of the spectrum.

"That's definitely the Illusion Card!" shouted Kero.

With a furious growl, Sakura raised the Sealing Staff, "Return to thine intended form, Clow Card!"

The fractal being shimmered as it dissolved into that stream of light. As it precipitated into a Card, Sakura felt a feeling of gratitude emanate from it. The sealing felt different from those she'd carried out before, as if she were a judge releasing a wrongfully accused man.

The air cleared, and the pool water started to settle, though it was only a quarter full. Sakura drifted toward her friends, and pocketed the Cards. Her face was expressionless for the moment, as she tried to come down off her emotional high. Tomoyo moved to put her hands on her friend's shoulders in an effort to comfort her. Kero just hung there in front of her. Both of them were silent save for the occasional awkward stammer.

"I'm glad," murmured Sakura. She sniffed back tears that could not be restrained. "It wasn't my Mum. She's not all alone in some dark place."

Kero smiled, and put his short arms as far around his master's neck as they would go. "'Course not," he cooed. "She's lookin' down with a smile and tellin' all the other angels, 'See? That's my girl!'"

Sakura gazed at Kero, and then turned to Tomoyo. Her friend had discarded the camera, and just stood with a reassuring grin.

Kero suddenly blurted, "And ya caught another Card! This calls for a celebration!"

No celebration could be had, unfortunately, as voices emanated from outside the gate. Lights in neighbouring houses had switched on, and police sirens blared from adjacent streets. Kero and Tomoyo started to panic, but not Sakura. She shot them a cocky look, and raised her newest Card.

* * *

Nothing out of the ordinary was to be found in the newspaper the next morning. Touya flipped through it and took note of new developments in Fukushima, more skirmishes with ISIS, and announcements from NASA's Mars rover. He did not see anything about an explosion at Sakura's school, or bothered neighbours. In fact, if he had had the mind to ask anyone near the school the previous night, they'd have said it was a nice, peaceful, uneventful evening – just the way they like it.

Sakura was rampaging around the second floor again, a herald that she'd overslept. But it was a weekend, so why was she so bothered?

"I'm going into town with Tomoyo today," she said as she wolfed down a few slices of toast.

"Well, be sure to say hi to Godzilla for me," said Touya with a sly grin. Sakura slapped the back of his head as she raced past him to bid good morning to her mother's picture. Touya smirked at his sister, but something else drew his attention. On the chair opposite him sat the lady in the photo, dressed in the same clothes Touya remembered her wearing every Sunday. The woman smiled at Sakura, who seemed not to notice her as she swivelled and raced out the door with an excited grin.

Touya's mouth was still wide with shock when the woman finally turned to him. He quickly murmured, "It's been a while, Mum."

"How are you, Touya?" said Nadeshiko. "Been studying hard for college?"

"Yes I have," he said with a formal tone. "And I've been looking after Sakura, just like you asked."

"Not always, though," said the woman. "I guess you can't be around her all the time."

Touya eyed the front door with a smile and said, "I at least know when she goes out to do her magic, and I can keep an eye on her from a distance."

Nadeshiko's smile widened, and her eyes drifted about the house. She sighed as the sights struck nostalgic chords in her soul.

"I might stick around for a while," she said. "I want to make sure Sakura will be alright."

Touya grinned, "That'd be nice."

* * *

A hat made of scaly leather fell to the floor of the dark warehouse. The girl with the purple tongue did her best not to wail as her limbs were twisted near to breaking point. Thick tears oozed out of her eyes as she pleaded for mercy from her invisible tormentor.

"I did my betht thoo kiw the candidate, mar-th-ter!" she squealed.

Suddenly, her arms were shoved right up behind her back.

"You athked me thoo tetht the wand in combat, and I did!" she cried. "How waz I thupothed thoo know Clow's staff would have prethidenth?"

Her eyes darted around as black sparks of electricity crackled along her aching limbs.

"But it waz jutht the Iwooshon Card, mar-th-ter," she cried. "I have the Shadow, Miwwor, and Thword. I can thtill defeat her."

Suddenly, her limbs were free, and she scrambled away toward a corner of the room. She held her hand tightly to her chest as she cowered defensively. She readied the serpent staff, expecting a fight at any second.

But her attacker wasn't anywhere in the room, except inside her.

6 | Shadows in the Alley

The bustling shops of downtown Tokyo appeared to the pair of girls as candy land to sugar-starved children. Being only fifteen years old, there was little they could afford. But just getting to gaze through the windows at the clothes, accessories, and latest music is plenty enriching for one's soul on a late spring weekend.

Firstly, Tomoyo led Sakura to the sewing stores. She promptly blew all her budget for their shopping date on books full of fashion concepts, much to Sakura's dismayed amazement.

"But I simply must have the best patterns!" Tomoyo exclaimed.

"Umm … Why?" asked Sakura.

Tomoyo struck a pose that would put Kero to shame, and she proclaimed, "So that I can make costumes that exemplify your cuteness!"

Sakura was content just to window-shop. She grinned excitedly as she eyed the red dress shoes in one window, adorned with pink ribbons. Then, she viewed the next window and shrieked with delight at the elegant summer dress. Behind her, Tomoyo had her camera at the ready, and with all the deftness of a sniper she caught her friend's every gleeful micro-expression.

As the day progressed, the tiniest tingle tickled at Sakura's earlobes. At first, she paid it no mind, but it eventually grew into a bother that distracted her from the merchandise she'd come to visually feast upon. Tomoyo could see her friend's mood.

"Is everything alright, Sakura?" she asked.

"I don't know," said Sakura with a furrowed brow. "I just feel a really strange sensation."

Tomoyo looked around cautiously, before whispering, "A Clow Card?"

"Nothing like that," she said. "Just an annoying sensation is all."

Takeshi's voice sounded behind them, and Sakura jumped as he suddenly blurted, "You know about 'sensations?'"

Sakura and Tomoyo swivelled to see the boy. His finger was raised as usual when he went on his spiels. He went on, "Sensations are when the hairs on your skin pick up vibrations."

"Vibrations?" Sakura echoed.

"Yep, vibrations," said Takeshi. His voice grew grave, "But these aren't vibrations like sound. They're vibrations of the quantum realm. And you can only feel them when you're shopping."

"Why is that, I wonder?" asked Tomoyo.

"They say there was a young maiden, who loved to shop," Takeshi went on. "But she eventually shopped so much, there wasn't anything left to buy. And her bags weighed her down so much …"

Sakura trembled, "Did she get crushed?"

"No, the sheer weight created a black hole, and dragged her into the quantum realm," Takeshi murmured. "It happened, right where you're standing. They say you can still hear her voice from beyond the quantum barrier, whispering …" He drew near to them, and Sakura and Tomoyo listened in closer.

"Whispering what?" they asked.

Takeshi murmured, "She whispers, 'Can I still get that discount?'"

Sakura was certain a ball of tumbleweed must have blown past them.

"What the heck?" she blurted.

Takeshi suddenly grabbed her hands and said, "Sakura, you should be my *tsukkomi*[9]."

"Don't go poaching my Sakura, Mister Yamazaki!" said Tomoyo sternly as she put herself between the two.

"Oh, I wouldn't dream of it, Miss Daidouji," said Takeshi. "Chiharu would kill me if I tried to replace her."

Sakura glanced over her protective friend's shoulder to ask, "So, where is Chiharu today?"

"She has some homework left over," said Takeshi. "I finished all mine, but she wouldn't let me help her. She said she wanted to do it on her own. Besides, it's her birthday coming up, and I wanted to get her something."

Sakura and Tomoyo's eyes lit up.

"What something are you going to buy?" asked Sakura, in part hoping she could glean some ideas for presents for Yukito.

"Hmm … I was thinking a bracelet of some kind," he said. "Care to help me pick? I'm not exactly good at these things."

Sakura and Tomoyo exchanged glances, and pondered a moment. Then Tomoyo had an idea, and she said, "I think there was an antique shop a bit back the way we came. Maybe they might have some very nice ornamental bracelets, and maybe broaches too."

The pair led Takeshi back down the street to the shop in question. The place looked old, in rustic European style architecture. But it was clearly a recent establishment by the smell that reminded Sakura of a new car. As they entered, a bell tinkled above their heads, and a kindly woman approached them from the counter.

---

9   In Japanese comedy duos, the *Tsukkomi* refers to the 'straight man' who corrects the *Boke*, or 'comic,' who often says something incorrect.

Sakura tried to keep her attention on the broaches Takeshi was reviewing, but it wasn't long before that annoying itch at her ears broke her focus. She started to wander about the shop, looking for something to keep her interest, but the itch just kept on bothering her. Tomoyo found her next to a shelf full of carved humanoid figurines, her eyes glazed over in a daze.

"Sakura, what's the matter?" she asked. Her hand veered toward her shoulder to shake her.

Suddenly, the shelf next to them creaked before toppling toward them. Sakura snapped out of her trance quickly enough to see it, and she threw her hands up to catch it. She and Tomoyo buckled under the sudden strain, but managed to push the shelf back up with Takeshi's help.

Sakura frantically scooped up the merchandise that had fallen. She apologised profusely to the woman, who simply raised her hand and said, "It's alright, dear. The figurines aren't broken, and it wasn't your fault the shelf fell. Things have been falling over all day."

Sakura's brow furrowed, "Does that happen often?"

"Only today, but I must say I put out a lot of merchandise this morning, and the shelves just might be overloaded," said the woman. With a glad smile she turned to Takeshi and said, "Would you like that sword broach, young man?"

Takeshi bought the broach he'd picked, and as thanks for saving her shelves the woman gift-wrapped it for him. He bade Sakura and Tomoyo good afternoon, and headed for the train station.

"I hope Chiharu likes her present," said Tomoyo, but Sakura still wasn't listening. Her bothered expression had grown into a truly irritated countenance, and Tomoyo said nervously, "What's the matter, Sakura?"

Before Sakura could respond, another voice interrupted them. A boy appeared behind them, not much older than them and dressed in a green Chinese style shirt with the top three buttons undone. A mop of dark brown hair framed a face dominated by amber eyes that shot deep into Sakura's. She withdrew slightly from his commanding presence as he murmured in a deadpan voice, "Are you Sakura Kinomoto?"

Sakura gulped, "Yes."

"Could I speak to you a moment?" said the boy, beckoning her toward an alleyway. Tomoyo gripped her friend's arm to stop her, but reluctantly followed. The boy awaited them in the shadow of the buildings lining the path. He pressed his hands together, and a light shone from within as he uttered a harrowing incantation in Chinese. The Shadow Key hanging from Sakura's neck suddenly glimmered as it floated out from under her shirt and wafted weightlessly in the air before her.

"You are the Master of the Shadow Key," murmured the boy with a disgusted sneer. "Internet videos, playing with the Clow Cards like toys. You have treated this like a game, and put people at risk. I, Emissary of the Lee Clan, hereby declare you an unfit master." He held out his hand toward the trembling girls and growled, "Hand over the Clow Cards!"

Sakura snapped out of her terror and gripped the Shadow Key tightly, "Never."

"Then I will take them from you," growled the boy as he advanced upon her.

Tomoyo promptly made herself Sakura's shield and shouted, "Stay away!"

The boy outstretched his hand purposefully, his index and middle fingers extended as he bellowed, *"Fēnghuá zhāolái!*[10]*"*

A gust of wind grabbed a screeching Tomoyo and threw her aside. She hit the brick wall with a thud, allowing the boy to charge Sakura unhindered. He suddenly hit an invisible wall, behind which Sakura held the Sealing Staff,

---

[10] Mandarin: "Wind Flower, Come Forth!"

with the Shield Card doing her bidding.

"Who are you?" she cried in between trembling pants.

"You needn't concern yourself with that," snapped the boy. He waved his bare hands about the air in front of him, before punching the barrier with a shriek. A wavefront of energy rippled outward from his hand and shattered Sakura's shield. The air between them vibrated with heat that knocked her onto her back. Her gymnast reflexes kicked in, and she used her momentum to flip back onto her feet. She quickly struck the Windy Card, the blonde sprite blasting from her wand and charging the boy. He merely grunted, before throwing out a flimsy piece of paper.

"*Chèxiāo*[11]," he commanded, and Windy promptly dissolved into her inert form. Sakura's jaw dropped in horror and amazement. The boy approached her slowly, muttering as he walked, "Your performance as a Clow Master is appalling. If you had just a fraction of the skill needed, you would not have fallen to a simple revocation spell."

Sakura backed away as she fumbled with the cards in her pocket. She finally found the one she wanted, and moved to cast out Illusion. The boy's hand grabbed her wrist, and wrested it violently above her head. He gazed down at her terrified face, and scornfully spat, "Weakling idiot! Treating something as dangerous as the Clow like toys? Making movies and showing off to the whole world? You'll doom us all! Now, give me the cards!"

Bash!

Sakura fell to the ground, her wrist sore and her brain frazzled. She watched as the boy hurtled through the air, flipping just in time to land on his feet. He nursed a bruised cheek as he glared at the man who stood next to Sakura.

"Touya!" she exclaimed.

---

[11] Mandarin: "Cancellation!"

"Get away from my sister, you creep!" roared Touya.

Undeterred, the boy wiped away a trickle of blood from his mouth, and assumed a fighting stance. Touya stepped forward and assumed his own, which made his opponent's eyebrows spike with interest. The boy barked, "Very well!"

He was suddenly airborne and twirling in the air as he hurtled toward Touya. Touya blocked his spin-kick with his right arm, and countered with a strike to the boy's side. The boy backed off to gain some more ground as Touya pressed his attack, throwing punches and uppercuts. He jabbed with his left, which the boy deflected to the right, and then swivelled to deliver a deft kick to the back of Touya's head. When his enemy hit the ground, the boy turned to Sakura, still a confused wreck on the ground, and charged her. He didn't get far before he found himself face-first down on the concrete, Touya's hand firmly locked around his ankle. The older boy threw him over his shoulder, before swivelling to make himself a shield for his sister.

The boy seemed quite dazed now, and only slowly did he manage to hobble to his feet. Blood flowed from his nose as he shot a death glare at Touya and Sakura behind him. Tomoyo came to her senses and shouldered her friend, as did another boy whom Sakura called 'Yukito.' When Yukito appeared, his face riddled with concern for the ongoing fight, the mysterious boy's expression changed. He then turned and sprinted down the alley. He darted off the walls, scaled a hanging drainpipe, and vanished over the roof.

Touya gazed after the boy a moment longer, gritting his teeth over what he saw in his opponent's expression. Even if Touya hadn't been the only one to see it, he would have been the only one who understood it, and it sent a chilly cocktail of bittersweetness and begrudging ire up his spine. He quickly shook it off and turned to Sakura, who stood trembling and sobbing as she clutched the Sealing Staff he knew wasn't a prop.

"You better not've been filming one of your videos with that creep," he said.

"We weren't filming anything," said Tomoyo. "We don't even know that boy."

"He just attacked us," Sakura stammered. Touya's heart melted, and his brow softened as he tussled her hair.

"Come on then, let's go home," he said.

Yukito leaned over to him, "Should we call the police?"

Touya scoffed as he gazed up at the roof to where the boy ran.

"Nah," he said. "That little creep ain't gonna try anything like that again."

* * *

When Kero got word of the attack, he was more furious and distraught than ever before. He bowled his master over and proceeded to search her up and down for scars and grazes. Of course, a flick to the forehead was increasingly effective to calm the Beast of the Seal.

He finally settled down enough to ask, "So, who was this brat?"

Sakura plonked down on her bed with a shrug, much to Kero's annoyance. Tomoyo's memory was sharper than Sakura's, and she said, "He called himself 'Emissary of the Lee Clan.'"

"The Lee Clan!" roared Kero as if it were the name of the Devil.

"Who are they?" asked Sakura.

Kero crossed his arms furiously and said, "Clow Reed, the creator of the Cards, was born of a British sorcerer and a Chinese witch. That witch was named Guanyin Lee. That brat's prob'ly a distant relative of Clow Reed."

Tomoyo stifled a giddy chuckle as she said, "The plot thickens!"

Sakura grabbed the Book of Clow and said, "Then, isn't this Lee boy right? Shouldn't *he* be capturing the Clow Cards?"

Kero shot her a grin as the book flew open and the seven cards that called her 'Master' encircled her. They glimmered as she gazed at them, smiling at their support.

"No way will these lot accept any other master, Sakura," said Kero. "You captured them usin' ya own powers." Nudging Tomoyo he added, "With a little help from your trusty side-kicks."

The cards fell into a stack in her waiting hands, and she heard their voices utter, "You are the master we want, Sakura."

Kero floated into the air and looked at her fixedly.

"This Lee kid, judgin' you ain't his duty," he said. "If anythin', he should be helpin' you. So, if he comes after you again, I'll smack him down."

Sakura beamed. She grabbed the Beast of the Seal and gave him a noogie as she cried, "Kero! You're so cool!"

Later that afternoon, Sakura sat watching TV, and was absolutely enthralled by the images of opulent European castles. More than once she wondered whether there was a Clow Card to make money, so she could become a princess and have such a castle. Of course, Touya was quick to dash her hopes.

"You could never have a house that big," he said. "Imagine the cleaning chores you'd have to do."

"I'm sure I'd have maids, just like Tomoyo," retorted Sakura.

"And then there's the fact you'd need GPS to find your way around," Touya added snidely. Sakura fumed and kicked him in the knee, but his grin did not waver. She moved to bicker further, but something caught first Touya's attention and then hers.

A news report had started during the commercial break, showing a woman being carried away by paramedics. Sakura recognised the injured woman as the antique store clerk. She watched, mortified, as the TV showed images of the woman's shop in shambles. All the shelves had been knocked over, with much of the merchandise damaged. Before she could ask what had happened, Sakura saw the video cut to an interview of the wounded clerk. Despite her injuries, she still wore a cheerful demeanour as she said, "I suppose I must have over-stacked the shelves and they fell off balance."

"That poor lady," Sakura murmured.

"Hey, that's right near where that creep attacked you," said Touya. "Maybe we should've called the cops."

"Well, she said it was an accident," said Sakura, though she was more concerned with keeping the authorities out of her extracurricular activities. Her eyes returned to the screen, and tingled as she noticed a flickering shadow in the corner of the frame. At first, she thought it was just an artefact of the transmission, but another shadow quivered elsewhere on the screen. Her skin broke out in goosebumps as she felt a sensation not unlike a Clow Card, as if the TV had digitised its magical signature.

Sakura raced out of the room and up the stairs to her bedroom, where Kero had just finished feasting upon a box of Tomoyo's cookies. She ignored the crumbs on the floor (that would normally infuriate her), and asked, "Kero, can any of the Clow Cards control shadows?"

Kero almost choked on his last mouthful of cookie.

"What do you mean? Did you see a shadow movin'?" he asked. Sakura described what she saw on the TV, at which Kero exclaimed, "Yep, that sounds like the Shadow Card. But it's weird for it to attack anyone. It pranks, sure, but not actually hurtin' anyone."

"Do you think it's the *other* Cardcaptor?" asked Sakura with a gasp. "Maybe it's that Lee boy."

"Wouldn't put it past the brat," spat Kero. "Call Tomoyo. We got work to do."

* * *

It was midnight in downtown Tokyo. The antique shop was empty, and the police had taped off the area. It give a three-person film crew a chance for some preproduction.

Sakura stood in a costume that made her look like Bat-Girl, with ribbons and dark floral patterns. She wore a dismayed expression as Tomoyo snapped picture after picture, with Kero in the foreground, a purple bowtie about his neck.

"You just wanted an excuse to dress up, didn't you?" Sakura murmured.

"The world must see my coolness!" Kero proclaimed as he struck another pose.

"What about Shadow?" Sakura asked meekly as Tomoyo adjusted her DSLR settings.

"We gotta wait for that brat to show up," replied Kero.

"In the meantime, I can get some test footage for our next video," added Tomoyo with a grin that was far too excited for the situation. She held up her camera and brought her models into focus. The flash lit up the alley, and Tomoyo saw that tiny flicker of a shadow, like a ghost, in the image. Sakura and Kero swivelled to face the presence they'd detected.

An umbral blade blasted out of the darkness, barely grazing Sakura's cheek. She darted out of the way and collapsed onto a stack of bins. Tomoyo backed away from the shadows with fright as a rain of black spikes flew out of the alley. The spikes sped toward the girl, and she shrieked in terror. Sakura appeared in front of her, the Sealing Staff conducting the Shield Card to hold the shadowy bullets at bay. When the ghostly machine gun finished firing, Sakura summoned her wings, grabbed Tomoyo, and carried her to the nearest roof.

"Sakura, it's definitely the Shadow Card, and somethin's controllin' it," said Kero.

Sakura threw out the Windy and Wood Cards and cried, "Wood, Wind, become binding chains!"

The Windy and Wood Cards burst forward in a storm of gusts and vines. They twisted and twirled about their opponent, but caught nothing but air. The shadow blades promptly ripped them apart, and they retreated to their

Card forms.

"He's too strong," groaned Windy in Sakura's mind.

"Fine then!" shouted Sakura as she threw out Watery. "Subdue the fiend standing yonder, Watery!"

The Watery Card morphed into its piscine form, and roared as it flooded the alleyway. A torrent of garbage bins flew across the street and smashed through windows and cars as they went. Water blasted at tremendously high pressure that Sakura couldn't control, and it ripped through the walls of the nearby buildings.

"Stop! Watery! You're breaking everything," Sakura cried, but her voice fell on deaf ears. She tried to reach out to the beast with her mind, but Watery writhed and thrashed relentlessly as it rampaged.

"Sakura, you gotta stop it!" exclaimed Kero. "Focus, girl! Focus!"

Sakura tried and tried. Her eyes started to sting anxiously as Watery savagely lashed out against her feeble efforts to still its mind.

Stop! Please, Watery!

"Pathetic!" barked a dreaded voice. Sakura, Tomoyo, and Kero turned to see Lee, cross-armed upon the roof railing. His face was still bruised, but only slightly, and it was twisted into a disgusted expression.

"Is this that brat who hurt ya?" exclaimed Kero.

Lee raised an eyebrow at the floating teddy bear, and he murmured, "It wasn't CGI? This fluffy thing really is Kerberus?"

"Who're you callin' fluffy, Brat?" barked Kero. "Hurry up and quit usin' Shadow!"

Lee scoffed, "This isn't my doing, Fluffy. I'm just here to fix your mess."

He marched forward, and grabbed Sakura's hand with his left as he raised his right. Sakura felt a pulse crackle up the nerves of her arm into her brain, and filled it with a sensation of vulnerability.

"*Chèxiāo,*" Lee roared, and the flood disintegrated into

beams of light that morphed into a Card in Sakura's free hand. Lee released her hand and glared angrily at her. "Your magical power is so weak a paper charm could revoke an offensive Card! You lack training!"

Sakura mewled at his verbal abuse. Her senses warned her of the incoming attack barely in time. She darted backward, tackling Tomoyo to keep her out of the path of the shadow's blades, which cut through the reinforced concrete wall behind them. Lee needed only lean backward, his eyes glued to her with a resentful glare.

"Well, you need to capture the Card, right?" he barked.

"Oi, Brat! Clear off her!" barked Kero.

Sakura wiped away her tears and said, "I tried to restrain it with Windy and Wood, but it didn't work. How do you capture it?"

"You gotta get at its core, just like with Watery," said Kero. Sakura's eyes darted side-to-side as she thought frantically. Part of her hoped, very much futilely, that she'd have another brain blast, like the snow cones. But none came.

"Think, you idiot!" snapped Lee, which only upset Sakura more. She couldn't bring herself to respond as she threw up her hands in surrender. That just infuriated the boy even more, and he leapt off the roof. He found his footing on a light post overlooking the spiny shadow beast. A paper charm appeared in his hands, and to it he murmured a Chinese incantation. Then he threw it upward and shouted, *"Léidì zhāolái!*[12]*"*

A flare of electricity impregnated the skies above in a flurry of vibrant sparks and arcs. Light flooded the entire block, and it ripped away the umbra that cloaked the spiky beast. There, exposed like an evil conspirator unmasked, stood a black wight that cowered in the light of Lee's spell.

"Seal it! Now!" he barked.

Sakura leapt onto the railing of the roof, and held up

---

[12] Mandarin: "Thunder Emperor, Come Forth!"

the Sealing Staff. "Return to thine intended form, Clow Card!"

The wight melted unceremoniously into a Card, before wafting into Sakura's hand. In between her bewilderment at Lee's treatment and her mellow elation at capturing another Card, she felt a similar aura of gratitude emanate from it. However, unlike Illusion, she could actually hear a faint whisper from the Card: "Thank you for freeing me."

She stood perplexed by the Card.

"I've never seen a sealing before," said Lee, as he leapt from his tall perch to the sidewalk. "But you now know, don't you?"

Kero was aware of it as much as Sakura, who stood dejectedly beside him on the roof. Even so, he stoutly retorted, "Know what, ya dumb ching-chong brat?"

"You're reaching your limits," said Lee. "So far, you've been lucky enough to meet the more cooperative of Clow's deck. And those were easy to sense and catch. But you've already demonstrated you're not up to the job. Shadow? That was only *one* of the Cards you missed today. From now on, the Card's'll only get tougher, and more vicious. Even if you manage to capture them, you won't be able to control them. Make a mistake like just then, and someone might die!" He pocketed his hands and started walking, not bothering to turn his head as he yelled, "Let me know when you're ready to hand over what is mine."

Even though she held a grateful Card in her hand, and two friends stood beside her trying to comfort her, Sakura couldn't hold back her tears of anxiety, distress, and failure.

7 | Harsh Criticism

For the first time in her life, Sakura didn't want to get out of bed. Instead of her usual scramble upon the alarm's screeching, she just flicked the off-switch on her clock and rolled over. Kero's pestering, followed by her father's call down for breakfast, finally dragged her out of bed.

"Don't let that brat bug ya, Sakura!" said Kero as he pulled her uniform out of the closet for her.

"I was useless," she droned. "All I did was mess the place up even more. I was lucky no one saw me and called the police."

"Sakura, the place wasn't that banged up, and the news said it was a broken water pipe," said Kero, patting her on the shoulder. "And ya caught Shadow too. Sounds like a success."

The dejected girl shot him an annoyed glare and said, "What happens when a Card comes along that's too powerful for me?"

Kero moved to console her, but she was already out the door. Downstairs, Franklin and Touya saw Sakura smile, but could intuitively sense her sad mood. At the very least, it staved off Touya's typical morning banter. Of course, Sakura would have preferred being called 'Kaiju' and the subsequent rage-induced aneurism that often followed.

She maintained that dour mood through the morning, though Yukito's presence did lift her spirits. By the time she got to school, she'd reached a mellow mood. Her cheerful state began to reassert itself as her friends gathered around for lunch and went about their discussions of current events. It even survived Naoko talking about the strange happenings surrounding the antique shop, thanks in part to Takeshi proceeding to explain how pipes used to be made of moulded salt crystals that kept dissolving.

By the end of the day, Sakura felt back to normal, with a dash of pensiveness. It was a welcome sight for Tomoyo, who grinned when she saw her friend smiling at the shoe lockers. Just as they were about to head home, Sakura pointed out Takeshi, who was hurrying to catch up with Chiharu a bit further down the path.

"Takeshi," Sakura called out. Then she whispered, "Did Chiharu like that broach?"

"She loved it," he replied with a grin. "Thanks for helping me pick it out."

"Not at all," said Tomoyo. "I guess she can't wear it at school, can she?"

"Uniform dress codes," replied Takeshi with a disappointed tone. Then he suddenly raised his finger pointedly, "Speaking of dress codes, did you know that, in the Harrapan Civilisation, if you didn't follow the codes, you could be put to death?"

Sakura's eyes widened, and she was instantly enthralled in the story. Before Takeshi could go on further, Chiharu appeared, grabbed the back of his collar, and dragged him away.

"He just can't help himself, can he?" Tomoyo intoned.

"What's the Harrapan Civilisation?" asked Sakura, at which Tomoyo just shrugged.

The walk home was, despite Sakura's renewed mood, much less talkative than usual. Tomoyo steered away from the Clow Cards, Lee, or their next video. However, this only made her realise how much the Clow Cards had consumed their relationship. Tomoyo could hardly remember what she did with her best friend before Kero came along. Just as Sakura's street came into view, it finally struck her.

"Hey, Sakura, when was the last time we had a bake-off?" asked Tomoyo.

"Hmm … I can't remember," said Sakura. She pondered a moment, before pursing her lips nervously. "If we did though, Kero would go crazy."

"Why don't we bake something nice today?" asked Tomoyo. "How about a cheesecake?"

Sakura's eyes lit up, "That'd be brilliant!"

Half an hour, two blocks of cream cheese, three eggs, and a pack of choc chips later, a truly gorgeous mixture sat baking in the oven. Three pairs of eager eyes gazed through the oven window at the concoction. Kero sat on his master's head and proceeded to fantasise about the taste, scent, and texture of the godly delicacy of which he was soon to partake. That daydream came to an end when Sakura felt his drool over her head.

"Kero! That's gross!" she exclaimed as she patted her hair dry with a paper towel.

"It's not *my* fault you decided to bake a cheesecake!" snapped the Beast of the Seal.

Tomoyo hung up her apron and made a pot of tea. Kero and Sakura continued their bickering, which eventually evolved into the more familiar rants about Kero's videogame addiction and his need for more exercise. Tomoyo was just content to sit sipping her tea, and let the sitcom unfold before her. Unfortunately, all good shows have commercial breaks, and the Sakura and Kero Show was no exception. A knock at the door halted their banter.

"Is that your bro?" asked Kero.

"He's not supposed to be back until late," said Sakura as she moved toward the door. When she left the room,

Tomoyo turned to the Beast of the Seal and said, "She seems to be back to normal."

"Yup! All she needs is a break from magic," said Kero as he half-filled his cup with tea and the other half with five tablespoons of sugar.

"Not too long, I hope," said Tomoyo with a sad look. "Otherwise, she won't be able to wear my costumes."

"I'm sure she'll get back in the swing o' things," said Kero. He suddenly dropped his tea as his head jerked toward the door. His face filled with horror, having sensed the attack before Sakura had a chance to scream.

Kero and Tomoyo raced to the entrance, where they saw Sakura on the floor. Standing over her in the doorway was Chiharu, in her hand a sword that almost made Kero faint. With a blank face, Chiharu sped forward, the sharpest point of the rapier vectoring toward Sakura's heart.

"No!" screamed Tomoyo. She raced forward and tackled Chiharu, cutting her arm on the blade as she pushed the swordswoman out of the door. She held up her charge, forcing the zombified Chiharu out the gate and onto the street. She tripped on the gutter, and fell on top of the attacker.

Chiharu targeted Tomoyo's throat, hitting nothing but air. She launched herself to her feet with the deftness of a master acrobat. She swivelled mid-air to confront Sakura, who stood shouldering her wounded friend. Ethereal wings fluttered from the girl's ankles, slowly fading as she brandished her Sealing Staff. Kero flew over to take Tomoyo off Sakura's hands.

"Kero, this is another Clow Card?" asked Sakura, her eyes glued to the attacker.

"It's the Sword Card," replied Kero as he strained under Tomoyo's weight. "It's controllin' ya buddy, so ya need ta get it outta her hand."

Chiharu sprinted forward, soaring above the ground toward her target. Sakura struck the Shield Card, but

Chiharu's blade flowed through it like tissue paper. She jumped back with a surprised shriek, and threw her arms and staff up reflexively. A twang of metal on a hard surface echoed along the street.

Sakura opened her eyes, and found that nightmarish amber glare boring into her. Lee's left hand was braced against the wall behind her, his right radiating magical ripples in the air between it and Chiharu's blade. The swordswoman gritted her teeth as she pressed against the magical barrier that did not budge.

"Useless weakling," growled Lee.

With a twitch of his fingers, he blasted Chiharu off balance before delivering a roundhouse kick. The force sent her down the street. Both Sakura and Tomoyo cried in horror as their friend hit the ground.

Lee's eyes were still glued to Sakura and he said, "I'll show you how to be a Cardcaptor."

Then he locked on Chiharu, who was now coming at him with the sword in hand. He leaned back to dodge her first swipe, and deflected her wrists to avoid the next. Chiharu thrust forward, aiming for his heart. Lee swivelled around the stab, swatted the sword out of the way and punched the girl squarely in the face. Chiharu stumbled backwards, and Lee ruthlessly pressed his attack, his every second and third blow connecting with the swordswoman's face and torso. Chiharu dodged a blow meant for her head, twirled and brought the sword toward his neck. He caught her wrist, slapped her hand from below, and grinned triumphantly as the sword left her hand and flew into the air.

The sword, it seemed, had waited for that chance.

While Lee was focused on catching the blade, Chiharu launched her own boxing attack. First, she got his exposed ribs, then his chest, before putting the sole of her foot into his stomach. She'd managed to push him out of the way enough for the sword to fall into her waiting hand behind her back.

The sword thrust home.

Lee flew backward, yelping in surprise as he flew head over heels. Chiharu fumed angrily at having hit his magical shield, raised at the last minute. Lee leapt to his feet, wiped away a trickle of blood, and said, "I guess I shouldn't try to fight you with my bare hands."

He opened his arms wide, and the palms of his hands began to glow. Then they flew together. Sakura landed in front of him and stopped his hands short of colliding.

"Out of my way, you idiot!" barked the Chinese magician.

"You can't hurt Chiharu anymore!" shrieked Sakura. She saw the swordswoman advance again, and with the Jump Card she dragged Lee into the air and out of the line of fire.

"If you want to seal that Card, you have to best her in a fight," snapped Lee.

"No," returned Sakura. "All I have to do is get the sword out of her hands. And I know just what to do."

Chiharu quickly turned on Tomoyo, who backed away frightened. Sakura put herself between the two, the Illusion Card at the ready.

"Embody the form of her dearest love, Illusion!"

Upon being struck, the Card morphed into an angelic hologram of Takeshi, his warm smile radiating into the swordswoman's eyes. Chiharu stopped dead in her tracks, her heretofore vacant expression filled to the brim with warmth. The sword fell from her limp hands, and Sakura saw her chance. She darted out from behind Chiharu's heavenly illusion and proclaimed, "Return to thine intended form, Clow Card!"

The sword vanished as a new Card appeared in Sakura's hand. Illusion also returned to its inert form, leaving Chiharu in a confused daze. She fainted on the footpath.

Sakura turned to Tomoyo, whose face seemed sunken from the pain of her wound. She gingerly pulled away her friend's hand to inspect the cut, which bled heavily. Tomoyo winced and twitched as she tried to hold back tears of agony.

"Dang! That looks painful," said Kero with a wince.

"Can any of the Cards heal injuries?" asked Sakura.

"None that you got," replied Kero.

"It's alright, Tomoyo," said Sakura, wiping away her own tears of panic. "We'll get you to a hospital."

"No need," growled Lee. Sakura swivelled, her face showing a glimmer of frustration as she cocked the Sealing Staff. What she saw surprised her. Lee held a paper charm over the bruises on Chiharu's face, which quickly healed. Then Lee approached Tomoyo, his hands held up in a show of peace. The girl cautiously showed him her cut, to which he applied the same charm. She inhaled sharply, like hot water had been poured over her skin, as the gash sealed itself.

His work done, Lee turned to Sakura and said, "You should take your friend inside and look after her. After all, you didn't recognise the Card when her boyfriend bought it."

Sakura frowned, "What do you mean? Takeshi bought a broach, not a Clow Card."

"If you haven't figured out that the Cards can disguise themselves, then you really shouldn't have this duty," replied Lee. "That was the second Card you missed the other day. I hope you're getting the picture, and will be ready to hand over the Cards soon."

He started to walk down the street, his hands in his pockets. Sakura shot to her feet and cried, "Teach me!" Lee stopped in his tracks, and Sakura went on, "Teach me how to use the Cards properly. That way, I can do better, and show that I am a fit master."

Lee stayed silent a moment, before looking over his shoulder.

"Impossible," he said. Then he turned a corner and was gone.

Chiharu came to not long after Lee disappeared. She rubbed her brow to shoo off her dreadful headache, and then looked around bewildered. Sakura and Tomoyo managed to convince her that she'd shown up for the afternoon, but accidentally slipped and bumped her head. Rather than calm her, the news just upset her.

"My broach is missing!" she cried. "Takeshi bought me that broach!"

She scrambled to the nearby storm drain to look for it, but only grew more distraught when she couldn't find it. Tomoyo whipped into damage control mode, throwing her arms around her friend to console her.

"I'm sure he'll understand," she cooed. "Yamazaki isn't so horrible as to get angry about a simple mistake." She turned to Sakura, who held the Sword Card and Sealing Staff behind her back. "Right, Sakura?"

"If you explain, he'll forgive you, Chiharu," said Sakura reassuringly.

The pair went inside to treat their distressed friend to tea and cheesecake. Sakura lagged a moment to look around for Kero, who seemed to have vanished. She couldn't linger too long before Chiharu started asking questions, and she just had to assume he'd flown up to her bedroom to hide.

He was hiding, but nowhere near Sakura's bedroom. When the front door shut, he floated out from within the front yard hedge, his dot-like eyes fixated upon the road down which Lee had just walked. They turned to the house a moment, and he pondered, "I gotta talk to this brat ... But, cheesecake." His lips pouted resolutely, "Nup! This trumps cheesecake!"

The Beast of the Seal took off after Lee's magical signature, though part of him wondered if he'd gone insane. That small portion of his soul, responsible for his saccharine addiction, bellowed in protest, *How could anything trump cheesecake?* The rest of his mind diverted all its energy away from the allure of sweets and focused it toward the pungency of Lee's signature. It was a scent he knew well, from long ago, when his brother and fellow guardian was still around. Tiny slivers of memory bubbled into his consciousness, reminding him of the last time he sensed such a lunar aura.

I almost don't wanna meet this kid, he thought as a soft tingle of grief tugged at his plush-toy heart. He shook his head and growled, "Gotta! For Sakura."

The trail led to a small block of flats near Yoyogi-Hachiman station: a brown speckled brick building, sandwiched between two white concrete blocks. The brat's presence wafted from the second floor unit like a rotten stench. Floating through the window, left open as if to welcome an anticipated guest, he saw Lee, seated in the middle of the unfurnished living room. An ornate magic circle of yin-yang symbols and elemental glyphs glimmered on the floor about him.

"You may enter, Kerberus," said Lee in Cantonese.

Kero drifted over and sat down upon the north symbol. With crossed arms, he said, "I'd hoped the Lee Clan wouldn't mess with my master's plan."

"To which *master* do you refer?" asked Lee.

"Clow, obviously," said Kero. "He intended for me to select the next master."

"That master would need to be judged, would she not?" asked Lee with a scoff.

"Not by *you,*" retorted Kero. "It is not the place of the Lee Clan to pass judgement."

"How about pre-judgement?" snapped Lee, his brow furrowed with frustration. "How about a second opinion, to see if the one you've picked really has the capacity to take this seriously?"

Kero's dish-shaped ears twitched irately, "She *does* take this seriously. *Very seriously.*"

Lee opened his mouth to retort, but an epiphany took root in his mind and restrained his voice. His eyes narrowed, and the irritation that had until then been directed at Sakura found its target right in front of him.

"She doesn't know, does she?" he murmured. By the look Kero shot him back, with a barely perceptible twitch of his eyebrow, Lee guessed the answer. He furiously growled, "No wonder she's unprepared. You've been coddling her."

Kero gritted his teeth furiously, "Says the brat who's been trained in magic since he was a toddler. Ya can't throw Sakura into the deep end."

"The Clow Cards *are* the deep end," barked Lee. "Weapons of the most dangerous, immense power, created by the incomparable sorcerer, Clow Reed. The DWMA, the Witches, even the Alchemic Regiment would sell their souls to get their hands on them. You let them fall into the hands of a girl who makes YouTube videos with them, and you don't even attempt to prepare her. Consider the consequences if she fails!"

The boy's eyes glistened with a certain type of fear with which Kero was very familiar. From that glare, the Beast of the Seal instantly understood he had made a mistake. He huffed to blow away the urge to smack himself over the head, but it didn't work. The feeling stuck to his mind like dried porridge to his fur.

Lee waited for some kind of response from the tongue-tied teddy bear, but none came. So he said, "You should convince her to hand the cards over to me, before they get too attached."

"No chance!" snapped Kero. "The cards want her, not you or anyone else."

"They'll have to change their minds," retorted Lee.

"No!" barked Kero as he shot into the air and glared resolutely at the boy. "Sakura *will* be the Master of the Clow. She'll pass the Final Judgement and win." He pointed fixedly at Lee, whose gaze was riddled with apprehension, and he bellowed, "You're gonna train her, just like she said."

"Like *I* said, it's impossible," replied Lee.

Kero roared, "She'll show you she can do it!"

8 | Doppelganger

The crater reeked of rotten eggs. The stench rose up from the jaundiced rock faces and stung the eyes of the purple-tongued girl. Her long tongue lashed out over her eyes to recover the water from her tears as she descended into the crater.

A gust of wind threw her around. The force was hardly worth comparing to what she usually experienced at the hands of her master. Regardless, it was unnerving, considering the place into which she was descending. It was hard enough maintaining her soul guard spell while flying – not an easy feat for a Witch of her meagre level – without having to deal with high altitude wind gusts in a volcano.

"I am here, mathter, *dopyuu*," she said to the being inside her. Her eyes scanned the walls of the crater, and she thought aloud, "Did it *have* to pick Kengamine Peak?"

Her small ears twitched, and she swivelled to see a few rocks tumble down the edge of the crater. There was nobody at the top of the hill; none but the best climbers and mountaineers would attempt a climb in early-May. Nevertheless, it sent shivers down the girl's spine.

"I underthtand, mathter, itz attwacted to hwot pwaithez," she said. Her glassy eyes scanned the walls of the crater, the serpent staff gripped tightly in one hand, a small packet of Clow Cards in the other. Suddenly, they stopped, having fallen upon a small crevice in the wall. With a soft whisper, "*Doppa dopya doppin!*" she hovered across the crater, and landed in front of the crevice. A warm draught blew from within the dark passage. It made her lick her swelling lips, and swallow vigorously to wet her dry throat.

"After thith, jutht one morw," she stammered, and then squeezed into the hole.

* * *

Spring was coming to an end, and summer was on its way. Just a few more weeks, and then there would be beach and pool. Not to mention it was not long before Sakura and Tomoyo got three days off starting on May Third, meaning plenty of time to make another video and do another bake-off.

So, why am I still down in the dumps? Sakura asked herself as she glared at her half-eaten popsicle. The rest of her body plodded down the street on autopilot as her gaze demanded answers of the frozen confectionary.

"Why do they call you *popsicle* in English, and *Iced Candy* in Japanese?" she asked. "You're sweet, sure, and icy. But iced candy? It sounds like the name of a rapper from America … Or one of David Bowie's rejected stage names." She looked to the sky and murmured, "Rest in peace, Dear Ziggy." Her eyes went back to the popsicle. "And the English word, *pop-sicle*. Are you an icicle that goes *pop?* Not really. You just kinda leave too much of a sickly sweet taste in my mouth when I'm done. Then you just make me thirsty, which is weird since you're supposed to be mostly water."

"Master?" murmured Windy, her inert Card form twitching in Sakura's pocket.

"What is it, Windy?" asked Sakura as she shoved the popsicle back in her mouth.

"You seem in a bad mood," said Windy. "Frankly, it's bothering us."

Sakura stopped dead in her tracks. The popsicle slipped out of her mouth with a little pop of her lips, which somewhat answered her earlier question. But she could hardly care about that anymore. Just in the tone of Windy's voice that only she could hear, she sensed how the Cards felt at that moment. She didn't like how it sounded.

Her mind drifted back to the last few days, following Chiharu's incident with Sword. Adding insult to the injury, Chiharu took far too long to calm down after losing her broach, and Sakura had to go into debt to Touya to buy her a replacement (and it wasn't remotely as nice). Then, she had to do all of Touya's chores for the week, leaving her with little time left to do her homework. Of course, it didn't help that Kero, after volunteering to do all her math drills, got every single question wrong.

As bad as all that was, however, it wasn't what got her worked up the most.

It was Lee.

He'd insulted her, made her feel helpless and useless, demeaned her, hurt Chiharu, and then refused to teach her how to use the Cards better. Her thoughts drifted to Watery, Shadow, Illusion, and Sword. Those Cards barely ever spoke to her, and when they did, she only ever heard grunts of negligible acknowledgement. She was sure it was because of her lack of magical skill. Lee could have helped her, but refused.

"Why is he so mean to me?" she asked aloud.

"Why is who so mean to you?" asked a beloved voice. Sakura swivelled to see Tomoyo, a warm smile on her face. It lifted her spirits.

"Oh, Tomoyo! You got out of club early?" exclaimed Sakura.

"There was a problem with the piano, unfortunately," said Tomoyo. "The teacher asked me to help her move some files, then I left." The pair began walking down the streets. The chestnut-haired girl's eyes grew pensive, and Tomoyo repeated her question, "Who were you talking about before?"

"Lee," replied Sakura with a resentful tone. "He could help me but won't. He's a meanie."

Tomoyo hummed, a mysterious grin smattered on her face as she gazed toward the end of the road. "He may come around in time. But until then, all you can do is your best." She patted her friend on the back, and Sakura smiled.

"Thanks, Tomoyo," she said.

Then Tomoyo blurted, "You must also wear my costumes!"

"For the love of God," moaned Sakura in English, her rolling eyes crowning a secretly excited grin.

* * *

The notebook sat open on the desk, three pages of it full of math problems, with the answers checked and all. Sakura leaned back and stretched, glad that, for once, she'd finished her math homework *before* 10 PM. Kero hadn't been much help – he rarely was – and had spent the last few hours on Sakura's laptop, pounding away at *Portal 2*. Now that Sakura was finished with her homework, it was dessert time, the only thing aside from an eyeball aneurism that could drag Kero from his video games.

Sakura descended the stairs, Kero playing dead on her shoulder, and turned toward the kitchen. The doorbell rang, but she paid it no mind as her father was already halfway down the hall to answer it. She opened the fridge and whispered to Kero, "What do you fancy tonight?"

"Sakura, could you come here a moment?" came Franklin's voice. It was stern, a tad confused, and unlike anything she'd ever heard before. She shut the fridge, ignored the moan from her shoulder, and walked to the front door. Two police officers stood in the doorway, business-like gazes directed at her.

"Are you Sakura Kinomoto?" asked the policewoman to her father's left. Sakura nodded nervously. The woman glanced at a picture, and then looked back at her. She finally said, "Can you account for your whereabouts this afternoon?"

Sakura shuffled under the piercing gaze of the police. "Umm … I walked home from school, since I didn't have gymnastics club this afternoon. My friend Tomoyo met up with me part way. We got here, Tomoyo and I chatted for a bit, and then she went home. And I've been doing my homework."

Franklin promptly interjected, "I can confirm my daughter was here all afternoon. May I ask what's going on here?"

The policeman stepped forward and murmured, "We have received a number of complaints of vandalism and destruction of property in Midtown, along with several charges of assault. Every witness gave a description matching your daughter. We even have security footage of one such incident, occurring at approximately quarter-past-five."

Sakura fell into a panic. "I didn't do anything! I've been here the whole time! I swear it!"

The policewoman held up the picture she'd been studying. The monochrome image clearly showed Sakura in the middle of Midtown Mall. From the pose, she appeared to be beating up a small boy and laughing while doing it.

Sakura's back hit the wall, and she shouted, "That is not me!" She glanced at her father, who wore a disturbed expression, and cried in English, "I didn't do anything like that, Dad, I swear!"

Franklin turned to the police and said unequivocally, "You have your answer, officers. If you intend to charge my daughter with something, I'll have to call my lawyer."

"You mentioned a friend?" asked the policeman.

"Yes, Tomoyo, she was with me when I got home," exclaimed Sakura, tears streaming from her panicked eyes. Franklin moved to her and enveloped her in his arms. He glared at the police as he cooed her, and his eyes said, "You've seen enough."

The policeman was convinced, his partner not so much. She said, "I have just one more question, Miss Kinomoto."

"One more," said Franklin curtly.

"Is there anyone else, besides your friend, who could corroborate your whereabouts?"

Sakura was still quite panicked. Her mind was frazzled with anxiety over being arrested and charged with attacking people. Her imagination, completely unruly when she was upset, threw out visions of an angry mob jeering her toward the electric chair. Somehow, through that tumult, she managed to conjure a vision of a popsicle in her hand.

"There's a convenience store, on the south end of Ochiai Central Park," she stammered. "I bought an iced candy there. The store clerk was really nice and let me have it for ten yen cheaper, since I didn't have enough coins."

The policewoman pursed her lips, studying the sobbing wreck of a middle-schooler a little longer. She finally said, "That'll be all for now. We'll interview your friend and this store clerk." As she strutted away, her partner bowed politely and said, "Please pardon the intrusion, Mister Kinomoto."

Franklin just nodded silently in reply.

"Miss Kinomoto, I'd like to say I believe you," said the policeman with a warm smile. "My kids are huge fans of you. I'm sure we'll get all this cleared up, and you can make more of your videos. We're all really excited to see Cardcaptor Sakura's next adventure." He gave one last bow, and then left.

* * *

The light of a full moon trickled through Sakura's window, and illuminated the floating silhouette of the Beast of the Seal. His tiny eyes glimmered with concern and sorrow as they gazed down upon the girl sleeping restlessly on the bed. He then gazed out the window at the silvery blue orb in the sky that outshone the stars.

"Yue," he mumbled. "If she can't handle this …"

Kero shook his head profusely to banish his bothersome thoughts. He reached out with his mind to the Book of Clow in Sakura's desk drawer. It released the Cards to encircle him.

Within their collective mind, the table was fuller than it was last time, though still as quiet. Watery sat to the side, his arms folded so tight water leaked from his soaked robes. Shadow and Illusion sat between Watery and Fly. Sword and Shield were on opposite sides of the circular table, and were dead silent.

So far, the only ones who spoke of their own accord were Fly, Wood, and Windy.

"The Moon Boy said there were other Cards," said Windy.

"Correction," murmured Wood. "He said our Master had missed Cards. So far there have only been two."

"And now there is a third," said Fly before returning to her grooming.

Kero's eyes scanned the room, overlooking the nose-picking Jump, and focusing on Watery.

"You got anything to say, Watery?" he grumbled.

"Regarding?" mumbled Watery with a sneer.

"Your actin' out the other day when Sakura needed ya," snapped Kero.

"I am what I am," returned Watery. "The Master's mind was an uncontrolled torrent, and so I reflected that."

Kero snorted, "Milgram'd[13] have a field day with ya."

He eyed Sword, and recalled its behaviour when it used Chiharu to attack Sakura.

Ain't unlike it, really, he thought, before turning to Shield and making the same mental comment. Then he

---

13   Stanley Milgram was a psychologist who studied people's willingness to commit terrible acts when commanded to do so by someone in authority.

regarded Illusion.

That barrier I hit that night, it wasn't Illusion's powers at all. No way. Illusion ain't a defensive or offensive Card. It's subterfuge. And what's more, it don't kill unless it's told to.

"Illusion," he said curtly. The spinning fractal glimmered in response. "You were ordered to kill Sakura, weren't you?"

"Of course not," Illusion purred with a dreamlike vibratory tone.

Kero's eyes narrowed, "I guess I should take that as a 'yes.'"

"I was ordered to take the Master on a holiday," Illusion insisted. "There were going to be cakes and mojitos."

Pathological liar ain't changed in a hundred years, thought Kero.

"I bore witness to the fact," mumbled Shadow in a long sonorous voice. "I can confirm that Illusion, Sword, I, and a fourth were captured by means of a counterfeit sealing wand. We were then set upon the Master."

"Who did it?" demanded Kero.

"We known't," said Sword, its blade shimmering as it trembled. "T'was a wraith most foul, with a soul gone awry with thirst for destruction."

"Yet that thirst was well tainted by fear," Shadow put in. "Indeed, the being that enslaved us was bent on ill will, but only by coercion."

"I thought she was sweet," chirped Illusion.

"Who was the fourth Card?" Kero snapped.

Shadow gazed to the empty seat between Illusion and Watery and said, "She who sits there."

* * *

Sakura spent the next day in a fit of nervous jitters. It was enough that the cops had interrogated her, but she had also to deal with nightmares of being trapped in prison, and then spend all day at school looking over her shoulder in case she saw her evil doppelganger. Tomoyo did her best to comfort her friend, even explaining that she corroborated her alibi with the police that morning. Her friends encouraged her to stay cheerful, and continuously reassured her that she wasn't the kind of person who could hurt anyone.

That, of course, didn't stop her from taking preventative measures.

Tomoyo called in one of her mother's drivers to pick Sakura up and take her home. Sakura sat in the front seat so that the driver would clearly see her. When they reached her house, she even took a picture of the driver and recorded his name on her phone, so that she could show it to anyone who came looking. When they got inside, she and Tomoyo plonked down on the sofa. Sakura was far too tired to think about magic, and just wanted to watch TV.

Not long after the girls found something to watch, Sakura heard her father arrive. She raced down the hall to meet him. He responded to her cheerful greeting with a brow knitted with confusion.

"Is Touya home too?" he asked.

"No, why?" asked Sakura.

"Well, I could've sworn that I saw you and him walking home through the park," replied Franklin as he leaned out the open door to glance down the street. When he turned back, Sakura was gone. She sprinted back down the stairs with her backpack and a mortified look on her face.

"I've got to go," she said curtly.

"What's the matter?" asked her bewildered father.

"I just realised I forgot to hand in an assignment at school!" exclaimed Sakura. She turned to Tomoyo, who leapt to her feet and followed her out the door. Franklin stood in the hallway, jaw ajar with confusion, and stammered as he noted Sakura's name next to dinner duty on the wall roster.

Kero flew out of her backpack as soon as they were out

of sight of the house, and fell in alongside his master. He eyed her terrified expression, but found few words to calm her. He piped up when he saw the entrance to the park two streets over.

"You sure your bro went in there?" he asked.

"That's what Dad said," replied Sakura.

"That other you that'd been goofin' around and messin' things up, whaddaya think it is?" asked Kero.

"I'd assume it's a Clow Card?" asked Tomoyo, who was slowly losing breath on account of not being a long-distance runner.

"If it is, you should be able to sense it, right?" said Kero.

Sakura screeched to a halt just inside the park, and scanned the area with her eyes and magical vision. Her internal dish pointed fixedly outwards in all directions, focusing on every single sensation she could discern. Then she felt a tingle radiating from her left, toward where the sun was slowly setting. But it was too vague, and the path in that direction split into three.

I need more focus, she fumed.

"Close your eyes," came Lee's voice. She turned and saw the boy, this time in a red shirt and blue jeans. His lips were pursed to suppress his sneer as he gazed at her. "Well, close your eyes and focus," he snapped.

"Can it, ya brat!" bellowed Kero, before Lee promptly grabbed the floating teddy bear and gagged him with his hand. He looked at Sakura expectantly.

Sakura did as she was told, though the boy's tone made her shudder nervously. That in turn diminished her sensitivity, and she lost the sensation. Her brow furrowed with frustration. Lee's voice reached her ears again, closer this time, and a little less strident than before.

"Calm down," he said. "Think about the sensation you know is a Clow Card. Recall the colour and scent. Now search for it here. Ignore anything that is not what you seek."

All sounds faded, all scents dulled, and all that remained was the buzz of silence. Only one thought echoed in her mind: *Where are you?* There was the tingle, and she locked onto it. Her mind's feelers reached outward to it, teasing out where the signature was the strongest, until she zeroed in on it.

Her eyes flew open as her outstretched finger went straight to her ten o'clock. She shouted, "That way!"

She sprinted, not caring whether anyone else could keep up with her, and bounded over bushes and around signposts. Under a tree, she found Touya's bag and bicycle next to a sign stating, "Warning: Cliff Ahead." The magical signature led her into the thicket beyond. She promptly cast the Fly Card, and soared over the bushes until she saw the edge of the cliff. A puff of kicked-up dust had only just started to disperse where Touya had hit the ground below.

"Touya!" she screeched in horror. She nose-dove to the foot of the cliff and found her brother, his uniform tattered, torn, and dirtied from his fall. He deliriously gazed up at the little girl who stood over him, wearing Sakura's face.

"You should stop looking like my sister," he mumbled, clearly unaware of Sakura's presence. "You should go back to your place in the sky where you belong." Then he passed out.

The doppelganger drew near to him, and Sakura roared, "Get away from him!" The doppelganger ignored her and covered Touya's face with her hand, cutting off his breathing. Sakura was knock-kneed with fear as the girl looked at her and whispered, "Please, help me!"

Rage filled her, and she cast the Shield Card. A translucent energy field enveloped her brother and threw back the doppelganger. The Sword Card went out next, its handle held tightly in Sakura's trembling hand as she veered it near the doppelganger's throat.

"Sakura, stop!" shouted Kero. She turned to see the teddy bear carrying Tomoyo to the foot of the cliff. Lee landed beside them. Sakura saw their pleading gazes, and grit her teeth furiously as she willed Sword to stand down. She looked fixedly at the doppelganger.

"Return to thine intended form, Clow Card!"

Nothing happened.

"What's going on?" she snapped.

"You haven't identified its true form," Lee explained. "Right now, it's doing as it's been told. You have to dispel the doppelganger's form before you can seal it."

"How does she do that?" asked Tomoyo.

"Figure out what Card it is," said Kero.

Sakura turned back to the doppelganger, which frowned angrily as she held her fists up before her chest. Sakura started back, expecting an attack, and then cocked her head as the doppelganger did the exact same thing.

It's mimicking me, thought a calmer portion of her brain that had started to push past her anger. She leaned forward to more closely study the being, which also leaned forward. *It's like a mirror image ... Wait!*

"You're the Mirror Card!" she cried. The doppelganger's guise melted away in a rain of ethereal shards to reveal a girl with long flowing navy blue hair, clothed in an elegant, similarly coloured kimono. She smiled, and threw her arms around a bewildered Sakura.

"Thank you so much!" she exclaimed. Sakura felt tears wet her shoulder as the girl sobbed, "I'm so sorry. She made me do it."

Sakura pulled away with a confused expression. "Who made you?"

"The Witch," said Mirror. "She found me first, and made me and my friends hurt you." She turned to Touya, unconscious on the ground, and murmured, "I'm so sorry!"

Sakura's heart softened, and she stroked the girl's cheek.

"Would you like a different master?" she asked. "I'll be nice, and never make you do horrible things."

Mirror beamed and said, "I would love that!"

With a grin, Sakura raised the Sealing Staff, "Return to thine intended form, Clow Card."

With a delighted sigh, the girl dematerialised and transformed into a Clow Card. Sakura took the Card, and breathed deeply to shoo away the rest of her anger.

Kero floated over to her and patted her head. "You did good, Sakura."

"We should call an ambulance for your brother," said Lee, whipping out his phone.

"What about magic?" asked Tomoyo. "Can't you just heal him?"

"You wanna explain how he came away without a scratch?" asked Lee.

Within ten minutes, an ambulance truck arrived with paramedics to assess Touya's condition. Sakura was glad to hear he hadn't broken any part of his spine, and it was just a twisted ankle.

The same dreaded pair of police officers arrived not long after the paramedics. The policewoman proceeded to interrogate Sakura regarding her brother's accident, though the girl was far more composed than the previous night. Tomoyo and, surprisingly, Lee's presence helped her nerves. And when the questioning was done, the policeman grinned at the Kero teddy bear rested on Sakura's shoulder.

"You two're real close, aren't you?" he said before leaving.

Sakura hopped onto the ambulance with Touya, smiling to Tomoyo and Lee as the truck took off down the road. When the truck was out of sight and the ravine was quiet, Tomoyo turned to Lee and said, "She really would like your help, Mister Lee."

Lee pursed his lips. "She's far too inexperienced. Kerberus should have selected someone else."

With a side-weighted smirk, Tomoyo grabbed his wrist and curtly said, "Come with me."

Tomoyo summoned her driver, who promptly arrived at the north gate of the park. She eyed Lee the whole way back to her mother's mansion, and noted how comfortable he seemed in the upper-class vehicle.

"Are all sons of the Lee Clan so used to being driven around?" she asked.

"The descendants of Guanyin Lee have been at the top of Chinese aristocracy since the time of Chin Shi Huangdi," said Lee. "We have guided the East through its trials and tribulations for generations, and all our family must be familiar with each of society's strata." He turned to Tomoyo. "This stay in Japan is supposed to be my experience in the middle class. Your school included."

Tomoyo's eyebrows rose. "You go to our school?"

"I transferred the week after my mother sensed the Clow Cards had awakened," said Lee. "Other parties are interested as well. So it was imperative I start supervising immediately. I only decided to interfere when I determined Kinomoto would not be a suitable master."

Tomoyo just smiled and gazed out the window. This intrigued Lee, who had expected some kind of rebuttal and vociferous defence from the girl. He waited a moment longer, but no such response came.

When they reached the house, Tomoyo greeted the maids warmly, and asked for tea to be brought to her video room. She then led Lee to what she affectionately called her *Sakura Shrine*. At first, Lee thought his Japanese wasn't up to par, and when she confirmed he heard her right, his brow furrowed with discomfort.

"Isn't that a little creepy?" he asked.

"I don't care how creepy it is!" exclaimed Tomoyo. "I simply must document the life of my beloved Sakura." She gazed out the corner of her eye, hoping to catch a bigger glimpse of what she'd only seen in tiny slivers on Lee's face. When she saw that subtle hint, she grinned.

That's jealousy right there, she thought.

"This is what I wanted to show you," she said as she

opened a file on her computer. A large projector switched on behind them and lit up the bare wall with a moving image of Sakura. She wore a bright pink costume with bows and ribbons. Two vibrant wings stretched out from her shoulders and carried her into the air.

"I've seen your YouTube videos, Miss Daidouji," said Lee as he crossed his arms.

"These aren't those," said Tomoyo. "This is the raw footage. Usually, we'll capture the Card, and then with the Card's help, reshoot a lot of the scenes to get it perfectly right. Mind you, we couldn't really do much about Watery, since he's rarely cooperative."

"That's an understatement," murmured Lee sardonically.

"What I wanted to show you was this," said Tomoyo, and she brought up another raw file. This one had slightly less quality, having been recorded by a drone. Lee was genuinely interested now, as evidenced by his raised eyebrows. He watched Sakura, in her blue jester costume, bounding around the Sunshine Aquarium and avoiding the security guards like a spy. An impressed smile tugged at his lips.

Her technique is flawed to be certain, he thought. *But there is definitely some skill there. If nurtured properly ...*

The projector shut off, and Tomoyo looked fixedly at him with a smile. "You agree?"

Lee scoffed before nodding acquiescently.

* * *

A soft tapping announced Sakura's presence. As always she was delighted when Yukito answered the door instead of her brutish brother.

He's a sickie now, so you gotta be nice, she reminded herself.

She walked in and set down two servings of pancakes on the bedside table before offering one to her brother and the other to Yukito. She smiled at both of them, doing her best not to turn pale at the cast over Touya's leg.

"You didn't put anything in these, didya?" grumbled Touya through a mouthful of pancake.

"How horrible! I made those especially for you," retorted Sakura. "And I'm doing your chores for you too."

"Hey, that's your debt to me," said Touya.

Sakura harrumphed. Then her ears started to tickle with Yukito's giggles.

"I wouldn't need to watch sitcoms," he said. "I could just come here and watch you two."

"Wouldn't need to watch King Kong either," retorted Touya with a snicker.

Sakura really had to try hard not to kick him. Luckily, she had her mantra: *One day, I'll find a Clow Card that'll make me bigger than a lamppost, and I'll stomp on him!* When she finished uttering that to herself, she noticed Yukito's attention focused on the teddy bear still on her shoulder.

"Oh, Kero's just keeping me company down stairs," she said gauchely.

"Do you need any help?" asked Yukito.

Sakura politely declined and sauntered out of the room. Yukito shrugged and went back to his fifteen-stack. He finished it before Touya was even half way through his three-stack.

"Got an appetite, don't ya?" said Touya, at which Yukito just smiled like the cat that ate the canary (and then maybe the canary's babies and babies' babies).

"Franklin told me Sakura raced out looking for you," he said. "She's looking out for you, so maybe you should go a little easier on her."

"Shaddup," said Touya. "I'll torment her as much as I like."

"And yet you'll defend her from that Chinese kid?" retorted Yukito.

"Only I get to torment her," growled Touya.

"Dude, you should seek help for that sister complex you got," said his friend with an incredulous grin. Not long after, he excused himself to find the restroom. When he was gone, another voice reached Touya's ears.

"I think he's right," said Nadeshiko, her ghostly form kneeling beside her son's bed.

Touya shot his mother a deathly glare. "You caught Sakura when she jumped out the window, but you couldn't stop me?"

Nadeshiko shrugged, "You work so hard all the time. I decided you needed a reason to stay off your feet for a while. I knew you'd ignore me if I told you to, so ..."

The boy winced at the jolt of pain going up his leg. He breathed slowly to bear the discomfort, and settled into a more comfortable position.

"Not exactly relaxing, Mum," he said. "Plus, you wanted me to look after Sakura."

"There's someone else who can fill-in for you," replied Nadeshiko.

* * *

Downstairs, Sakura finished washing up the last pot, which she handed to her doppelganger to dry. When everything was cleaned and stowed away, Mirror morphed into a Card and teetered its way into Sakura's pocket.

"It's real nice having a Card like that," she said. When no response came, she looked over at Kero on the bench top, sound asleep. "You're not exactly helpful with chores, are you?" she murmured.

Before she could rouse the lazy creature, her phone buzzed. Lee was on the other side of the call.

"Kinomoto, do you want to become Master of the Clow?" he asked sternly.

Sakura huffed resolutely, "Yes."

Lee then replied, "Then I'll train you."

9 | In the Forests of Tokushima

Lee said he'd train Sakura, but only during the school holidays, and only in a remote location. So she had to wait.

The weeks were hardly uneventful. Another Clow Card, Flower, had shown up at their athletics carnival. She'd nearly drowned the school in flower petals before Sakura caught her. Not to mention, Sakura had managed to push her grade up a notch in the final weeks, which had been key to convincing her father to let her go on a hiking trip with Tomoyo.

That trip was just a cover, though. In reality, she was going to Shikoku to meet Lee, and train to become the Master of the Clow.

The hour-and-a-half flight from Tokyo, complements of Lee, was only the quickest part of the trip. Sakura and Tomoyo managed to snag a flight that was mostly empty, so Kero was able to fly around, and they each had a row of seats to themselves. Tomoyo had taken that time to triple-check all the recording equipment safely stowed in her backpack.

Takamatsu Airport was much smaller than the glorified shopping centre and hotel of Tokyo Haneda. That made Sakura breathe a sigh of relief, made even more pleasant when she entered the arrivals gate and realised nobody recognised her. As opposed to the onslaught of YouTube fans at Tokyo Haneda, it was a very much welcome change.

"Oh, but when my Dear Sakura becomes a star! Shall it not simply be the epitome of joy?" exclaimed Tomoyo upon hearing Sakura's verbalised thoughts.

"I just hope that no one in Tokushima recognises me," said Sakura. She then leaned over to whisper, "Trekking through the woods."

They hoisted their packs onto their shoulders and began walking. Sakura cringed a little when they passed by the taxi rank and the shuttle busses. But Lee was adamant when he said, "Take any transport other than the plane, and I won't train you."

"Dumb brat, the heck he think he is?" growled Kero silently from Sakura's shoulder.

"He said he'd train me, and I guess this is a warm up," said Sakura. Then she added, with her thoughts pointed at the cards, "Plus, I'm sure my friends will happily help me out?"

"At the ready," said Windy and Wood.

Still the only ones speaking to me, thought Sakura with a huff.

A brief walk north took them out of the airport, before a left turn led them around south and into a tunnel going under the runway. Now that was quite the shudder-provoking experience for Sakura. Of course, it didn't help when Kero mumbled, "It's like a scene from Marble Hornets."

"What's that?" Sakura stammered as she clung to Tomoyo's arm.

"Series on YouTube," said Kero. "There's this bit where they're in a tunnel, running from the ghost of Slenderman, and then *boom!*"

Sakura jumped five feet in the air and raced the rest of the way down the six-hundred-metre tunnel. She met the exit with an overjoyed sigh, but then had to wait while the less-fit Tomoyo caught up. Then, they continued east through Nagano, then south along a highway. The trip was pockmarked by jokes, chatting, and even a chorus of *Catch me, Catch you*. The hike was so much fun that neither Sakura nor Tomoyo noticed the growing soreness in their feet or the dwindling levels of their water bottles until they stopped for lunch at an udon place near Nakagesho. Only then did they check their watches and realise they'd been walking for four hours, and weren't even close to their destination.

"Aw, come on!" exclaimed Kero as he devoured the takeaway udon Sakura had bought for him. "You sure ya GPS ain't messed up?"

"Nope, I've checked a couple of times," said Tomoyo, red-faced with exertion. Sakura just rubbed her tired face as she gazed down the road with a bewildered expression.

"How much further then?" snapped Kero.

"About another sixty kilometres," murmured Tomoyo sheepishly.

"This is a test," Sakura concluded. She stomped the ground, swivelled and lifted her backpack. She momentarily eyed the sun veering west, before she said, "Come on then, let's get going. Should get there sometime after dark."

Another five hours of walking.

There was far less jovial chitchat or singing, and more banter of the complaining kind. Much of it was Kero, griping about Lee's behaviour and lamenting not being given Sakura's phone to play. Tomoyo remained the more cheerful of the three, and always filled their water bottles with a smile beneath which her pain simmered. Sakura, by contrast, was quiet and pensive. During their frequent rest breaks, she sat silently, her eyes fixed forward and her hands held meditatively.

I will do it, she thought. *I'll definitely win.*

The sky had turned bright red as they crossed the Yoshino River, on the boarders of Kagawa and

Tokushima. That lifted their spirits considerably as they set their seemingly much heavier backpacks down and took a break to watch the view. The sun was still a very bright white that slowly bled into orange and red as it crossed the sky above them.

Even if we don't meet Lee, this sight's worth the hike, thought a smiling Sakura.

The walk into Tokushima went on for another hour and a half, well after darkness had taken the world. Be it the fatigue, the dwindling battery in their phones, the lack of water, the burning pain in their feet, or lazy Kero snoring on her shoulder, Sakura hit her limit.

"How much further?" she droned.

Panting, Tomoyo took out her phone – its battery indicator at five per cent – and checked the map. Her tired muscles drained when she saw the figure on the screen. "Another ten hours!" she cried.

Completely fed up, Sakura growled, "Fine!" She reached down the front of her shirt, withdrew the Shadow Key, and roared, "Release!" The Sealing Staff materialised in a flash of light sure to wake the residents of nearby Yamakawacho. It certainly woke Kero.

"What's up?" he moaned.

"It's too far, so we're flying the rest of the way," said Sakura.

"Isn't that against the rules?" asked Tomoyo.

"Lee said we couldn't use any transport," said Sakura, a glimmer in her tired eyes. "But he didn't say anything about using the Clow Cards."

Sakura struck the Fly Card and summoned those wings to her shoulders. Then she put her arms around Tomoyo.

"Ready?" she asked determinedly. Her friend could only smile nervously.

"Hang on, Sakura!" exclaimed Kero. "It's gonna be thirty kilometres, *at least*. Fly can't go that far!"

"Not if I help," said Windy, who floated from her pocket. "I can create a sturdy gust."

"Sounds good," panted Sakura.

"Gah! This is so dangerous!" exclaimed Kero as he gripped Sakura's backpack. Sakura began to flap her wings, a far more laborious action than usual. Slowly, she and Tomoyo rose above the hills. They would have been very conspicuous to anyone in town that might have been looking outside at the time. They lingered there a moment as Sakura shuffled Tomoyo's weight. That only made Tomoyo even more nervous than before, as her eyes involuntarily darted downward to the ground far below.

Sakura held out the staff to the Windy Card, floating patiently like an eager cadet in parade, and murmured, "Become a sailor's perfect wind! Windy!"

The Card transformed into that magestic sprite. She shot behind her master, and came about at breakneck speed. The shock blasted the trio through the sky, across the landscape. Sakura, Tomoyo, and Kero all let out screams that the rushing air forced back into their lungs. Not a good thing for the disturbed and tired Kero and Tomoyo; a terrible idea for the mentally drained Master of the Clow.

Suddenly, the wings vanished, and the winds quieted. Gravity reclaimed them just as Tomoyo saw her unconscious friend, and started to scream. The softly moonlit ground rushed to meet them as an over-amorous friend comes to give a crushing hug. In a panic, Tomoyo desperately tried to wake her friend, while Kero tried to pull on Sakura's backpack to stop their fall. Hope was fading, and Tomoyo wailed with frenzied despair as their dreadful final landing zone came into view. She squeezed her eyes shut, gripped her friend tightly, and begged for a saviour.

* * *

Sakura opened her eyes and found herself curled up in a sleeping bag. A dim yellow light seeped through the tent's material, signifying daytime. She stretched and yawned, after which her brain finally decided to replay it's last memory.

That's weird, she thought. *I don't remember setting up camp. I was flying ... Right?*

She wriggled out of her sleeping bag and left the tent. The chirping of birds in the trees and the cracks of twigs by foraging animals were clearer in the open air than in the tent. The scents of the forest filled her nostrils, doing a much more pleasant job of waking her than her alarm clock. Another scent crept into the mix: smoke.

A bit further down the hill, in a small clearing, Sakura could see Tomoyo tending to an open fire. She hopped down toward the clearing, cracking twigs signalling her approach. Tomoyo turned and beamed at her arrival.

"Good morning!" she said.

Kero floated into the air, a bowl and chopsticks in his hands, and through a mouthful of rice gruel he said, "Get enough sleep?"

"Plenty, thanks," replied Sakura. Her eyes darted around a moment before she added, "I don't remember getting here last night."

"That's because you passed out," bellowed Lee. Sakura looked up to the source of his voice, and saw the boy standing upright on a branch high above the ground. His face still radiated a judgemental glare that Sakura, quite frankly, had grown tired of seeing. He hopped off the branch and slid down the height of the tree, his hands held to its bark by the softest clenches of his fingers.

"I only passed out because you made me walk all the way from Takamatsu," exclaimed Sakura. "I was so tired I couldn't take it any longer."

"So you decided to use Fly," said Lee. "It was a good idea to use Windy. But it was obviously too much for you."

Sakura folded her arms irately, and snapped, "So, you're not going to train me because I didn't pass your insane test?"

"No, not at all," replied Lee as he served himself a small bowl of rice gruel from Tomoyo's pot. "I'll train you. It's why I brought you here. I just wanted to test your stamina. To be honest – " there was some genuine admiration to his tone " – you did a lot better than I expected. The fact that you managed to use Fly and Windy at the same time, even though you were so fatigued, means you have way more power than I thought. I almost couldn't keep up with you."

Tomoyo pursed her lips in annoyance and said, "When you passed out mid-air and started falling, he saved us with his wind magic. We landed just at the bottom of this hill."

"This brat was followin' us the whole time," snapped Kero, who had become a ball with all the rice gruel.

"Like I said, I wanted to test your stamina," Lee rectified. "And you passed. So now we can begin the real training."

Lee made a call to someone on his phone. Then he sent Kero and Tomoyo off down the hill toward the road, telling them that a driver will be there to take them to Monobecho for supplies.

"Get protein supplements," he said as they begrudgingly left. "We'll need them."

Then, he led Sakura to the top of the hill, allowing her a chance to see the landscape. Deep valleys lay either side of the hill, which rose between them like a blade. Only in the furthest distance could she see the blurry mirage-like signatures of towns and villages. Fields of forest lay before her, softly buzzing with the sounds of birdcalls and branches ruffling in the wind.

"How far into the forest are we?" she asked.

"Up north, that way," said Lee as he pointed to a peak on the horizon, "That's Mount Kumoso. Takamaruyama is to the east."

Sakura shot him a confused look. "I don't know what those are."

"We're near Ogama Falls," said Lee. "This place is

remote enough that we can train without any disturbance. Though, I'll bet your friend will insist on filming some of our work for her next video." He hopped onto a rock at the peak of the hill and proclaimed to her, "Don't let it distract you."

"I won't," said Sakura determinedly. "I will be Master of the Clow."

* * *

I don't wanna be Master of the Clow!

That became Sakura's thoughts at the end of every day of training as she fell on her back, exhausted and sore. Her muscles ached as if they were being stabbed in certain places by tiny knives, and her head spun from fatigue.

Lee made her run up and down the hill five times a day, and then made her do hundreds of push-ups and sit-ups. There was no mention of magic except, "Your physical strength needs to be built up before you can learn magic." He assured her the protein shakes Tomoyo prepared would help with the muscle pain, but more and more Sakura just felt like he was trying to coerce her to give up the Clow Cards.

What kept her going each day were the SMS conversations with her family back in Tokyo – especially Yukito. Of course, she didn't tell them she was doing rigorous magic training; just hiking. But being able to talk to them, even in text form, was uplifting enough for her to meet Lee's increasingly insane demands.

That came to an end one day when she took a little too long on the phone with Yukito. He was talking about the newest record from BabyMetal, which had Sakura really excited. She was so enthralled in talking about the band, she didn't notice Lee approach her from behind and snatch the phone from her hands.

"Hey! Gimme that back!" she shouted as she lunged for it. Lee swatted her hands out of the way as he checked the phone.

"This is that Tsukishiro boy?" he said with a smirk. He began typing.

"What are you messaging him?" Sakura screamed as she launched her attack to reclaim her precious phone.

"I'm telling him you've got to go," replied Lee, delivering a light but firm palm strike to her chest, which sent her stumbling into a tree.

"Oi, Brat!" bellowed Kero as he flew through the trees toward them. "Don't be beatin' up Sakura, ya hear!"

Lee pocketed the phone and glared at the Beast of the Seal. "She's distracted in training."

Kero fumed, "You'd better treat her right!"

"Or what?" spat Lee with a sneer.

Kero threw up his tiny dukes, ready for a fight. Before he could even advance, he heard Sakura's voice, riddled with fury he'd never heard her express.

"Release!" she cried, as the Sealing Staff appeared in her hand. She struck the Wood Card, which summoned all the branches from the trees either side of Lee to charge him. He darted out of the way of one volley, and swatted another aside. His face expressed anxiety as he threw out one of his paper charms and cried, "*Chèxiāo!*"

The branches didn't vanish at first. Rather, they seemed to hesitate, as if unsure whether to disintegrate at Lee's demand, or continue fuelled by Sakura's determination. They finally erred on Lee's side, and disappeared. Frustrated, Sakura pulled another Card, but Lee caught her arms before she could strike it.

"Enough," he said calmly. Sakura struggled a moment in his grip, but eventually acquiesced and relaxed. She looked into his eyes, and saw him very slightly smiling. It wasn't a warm one like that of Yukito or her father. In fact, it seemed more like one of Touya's evil grins whenever he was teasing her. His smile widened as he stepped back and eyed her phone in his pocket.

"Come with me," he said. He and Sakura trekked back to the top of the hill, leaving Kero floating in mid-air, gritting his teeth at the situation his master had fallen into. Tomoyo approached him, having covertly recorded the whole thing. She had a mysterious grin on her face.

At the top of the hill, Lee turned to his pupil and said, "Magic is all about intention. You must very clearly be able to see your objective in order to achieve it. With the Clow Cards, it's even harder. Not only do *you* have to be able to see your objective, you must also make the Cards see it. It's not enough to simply state it, either. You must be able to communicate it directly into the Card's mind."

"I try to do that," said Sakura. "I do it all the time with Windy and Wood."

"Of course," said Lee. "Those Cards are nice, and have the most in common with you. But a Card like Watery, you already know is very different. You are very different from him. He's violent and ruthless, like a wild bull."

"I've used him before," said Sakura. "I was angry at Illusion for impersonating my mother." She added with a self-reflective glimmer in her eyes, "I'd never been so angry before."

"Exactly, your anger resonated with Watery, and it knew your intentions instantly," exclaimed Lee.

"So I need to get angry to use certain Cards?" asked Sakura, concerned about becoming violent.

"No, you simply need to match your soul's wavelength to that of the Card you're using," said Lee. "I've been training you hard, yes, to increase your strength and stamina. But also I was pushing you to get angry over something you care about." He took out the phone and scanned through the photo library until he found the image he wanted. With a sly grin, he said, "I am going to teach you a skill called Soul Resonance. And I'm going to do it with him."

He showed her the picture he found on the phone. It was Yukito's smiling face. Lee's own grin widened when he saw her swoon, and said, "When you have been trained, you may talk to Yukito."

* * *

Each morning after that was a bit of the same: run up and down the hill, followed by push-ups and sit-ups. Afternoons, however, seemed to be completely different. Instead of more painful exercises, Lee preferred games resembling cat-and-mouse.

One day, he bounded over the treetops while Sakura had to catch him with Wood. She had to admit, it got a lot easier to control the branches when Lee taunted her with Yukito's picture. But she never managed to catch him.

Another day, he put her phone on the ground and came at it with a heavy rock. Sakura used the Shield Card, and had to focus her mind to block the attack from different directions. Lee managed to chip the side of her phone – luckily the screen wasn't cracked. Then he had her do it again, this time imagining that it was really Yukito she was protecting. After that, Lee didn't land a single blow.

Lee spent some time teaching Sakura hand-to-hand combat drills. After she'd grown a little proficient at it, he then had her cast Mirror and make her doppelganger match her every move exactly. That took a bit of work, since Mirror tended to do the mirror-image action, so Sakura needed to think the opposite of what her body was doing.

At dusk, one day, Lee decided to have another one of his hide-and-seek games with Sakura's phone. He'd managed to dodge her attacks with Wood and Windy, though it was getting harder. Then he saw Sakura's shadow out the corner of his eye and darted northward away from it. But then he saw the girl's shadow in front of him, and had to turn away. He leapt onto another branch and found himself falling straight through it as it vanished in a flurry of fractal colours. The phone fell out of his hands as he lunged for one of the lower branches. His hand found a solid alcove to grab, and he looked down to see the phone falling into Sakura's waiting hands.

"*Shuǐlóng zhāolái!*[14]" he roared. A blast of water flew from his outstretched fingers, and hit Sakura squarely in the face. She tumbled to the ground with a shriek, and rubbed the water from her eyes. She looked up to see Lee standing over her, the phone in his hand, and a triumphant smirk on his face. She shot him back a playfully begrudging sneer.

"Watery!" she cried. The Card launched a spray of water that knocked Lee on his back. Watery's piscine form knocked the phone out of his hands, and then held him against a tree while Sakura raced to catch her prize.

Almost got it, she thought excitedly. Unfortunately, that broke her resonance with Watery, who vanished into a Card just in time for Lee to swat Sakura's hand out of the way and catch the phone. The sight made Sakura growl like when she would plot vengeance against Touya for a prank.

On the Saturday of the second week of their trip, Lee didn't come to Sakura's tent. She overslept, and upon waking up, she went to the top of the hill, where Lee was silently meditating.

"Lee, aren't we training today?" she asked.

"Nope," replied the boy. "You're having a day off. Tonight, I'll begin your final lesson."

"Why tonight?" asked Sakura.

"No reason," he murmured.

Sakura considered going back to camp to help Tomoyo with breakfast, since her friend had done nothing but cook for the two of them while they trained. However, something pulled her toward the boy, and she decided to sit down next to him.

"I'm not giving you your phone," he said curtly.

"That's alright," said Sakura, though her lips pursed with annoyance. "I just suppose, if we're not going to train today, why not have a chat?"

---

[14] Mandarin: "Water Dragon, Come Forth!"

Lee opened his eyes and turned to her, one of his brows raised. "Chat about what?"

"Well, what're your interests?" she asked with a shrug. "Obviously, you don't like meditating and training all the time."

Lee cocked his head and thought for a moment. "I suppose I like a good game of poker."

"You gamble?" asked Sakura nervously.

"No, just playing," said Lee. "I did that with some friends on exchange in America."

"Oh, you can speak English?" asked Sakura. She switched languages. "So you can understand what I'm saying?"

Lee nodded, though his eyes radiated surprise. "You have a British accent," he replied with a Californian accent.

"Dad's from Britain," said Sakura.

"But, your surname is Kinomoto," said Lee, his brow knitted with confusion.

"Mum's name was Nadeshiko Kinomoto," said Sakura. "He took her name and moved to Japan with her."

"Sounds like a nice guy," said Lee. "My father's quite strict. He expects a lot from me and my sisters. My mother does too."

"But he's nice, right?" asked Sakura, envisioning an authoritarian figure with a lash.

"Oh, of course he is," said Lee. "He just prefers I study hard rather than watch movies."

Sakura giggled, and said, "What kind of movies do you like?"

Lee scratched his head as he scanned his memory. "I like anything with Jet Li."

"*Lethal Weapon Four?*" asked Sakura with a wide grin. Together, they said in a sinister voice, "In Hong Kong, you be dead!" The recitation had Sakura laughing hysterically, while Lee was much more reserved in his chuckles.

"I'd never thought a girl like you would like violent

action movies," exclaimed Lee.

"My brother would make me watch them," said Sakura. "He's such a meanie. He once made me watch *Alien*, and then he made me watch *Shingeki no Kyojin*."

"You think you got it bad?" retorted Lee. "My eldest sister made me watch *Poltergeist* when I was three. And then all the *Ring* movies."

Sakura shuddered at the thought. She thanked her lucky stars that her father had intervened when Touya tried to make her watch those movies. She probably wouldn't have been a Cardcaptor if she'd seen more horror movies.

A sudden click made Sakura jump three feet in the air. Her nerves, heightened by talk of horror movies, made her swivel on the rock and take a fighting stance. Lee also turned around, with a more disinterested demeanour, and saw what she saw: Tomoyo with her DSLR and a wide grin.

"Taken enough pictures, Miss Daidouji?" asked Lee.

"Ah! It's like a confession scene from a girl's comic!" exclaimed the paparazza. "I think Tsukishiro has a love-rival!"

Kero shot up from behind her and roared, "Not on *my* watch! Sakura, you start dating this brat and I'll disown ya!"

Sakura fumed with embarrassment and yelled, "We weren't doing anything like that. I was just trying to get to know him better."

"And I didn't do anything untoward," said Lee, his hands raised though his face showed some sincere amusement with the situation.

Sakura proceeded to chide Tomoyo and Kero about their stalker-like habits. Tomoyo replied with more giggles and stabs at Sakura's shyness, while Kero continued to berate his master. They were all caught up in their foil argument that only Lee noticed the sudden encroachment of a bizarre sensation. It was so quick and powerful in its appearance that he didn't recognise it until Sakura sensed it too. Her heart skipped beats at the magnitude and voracity of the presence.

The sky turned dark, the landscape faded, her friends vanished, and Sakura was alone.

10 | Soul Resonance

In the void hung the Beast of the Seal. The strands of his fur simmered with the faintest hint of his true power, yet even that light was dulled by the darkness around him. Though he could not see his master, he could feel her aura vibrating through the dimensional folds of the void, concealing her light but not her presence.

"This is it, Yue," murmured Kero. "If she can't handle this …"

Lee stood before him, and could also sense the presence of the Master of the Clow. His calm consciousness wafted an air of mental control enough to withstand the void. However, it paled in comparison to Kero's glow, and he appeared as little more than an outline of reflected starlight. His amber eyes glimmered as they met Kero's.

"You wanted a chance for her to show me," said Lee. "Now she can."

And though the outermost reaches of his consciousness were as a still pool of water, the clenching of his jaw showed clear as day: he was terrified.

* * *

Pitch black enveloped the horizon, the sky above, and the ground below Sakura's feet. Her skin broke out in goosebumps at the sudden onset of cold.

"Tomoyo! Kero! Lee!" she screeched. When she screamed, not even an echo returned to her ears. The darkness voraciously consumed all light and sound. Sakura's eardrum's jittered with the hum of silence.

This is a Clow Card, she thought as she recalled the sensation she'd detected earlier. Her legs still trembled at the sheer magnitude of the presence and the speed with which it had snuck up on her. Her mind went back to that sight of Lee's face just as the blackness consumed him: surprise, alarm, and something she'd never seen him express – fear.

He knew what Card it was, I'd bet, she thought. *But I can't ask him, since the shadow's got him.*

"This isn't Shadow, is it?" she shouted, partially expecting Lee's voice to return to her from a distance. Another part of her was asking the void itself, as if it had anything to say to her.

No, hardly any of the Cards have anything to say to me, do they? Besides Windy, Wood, Fly, and Jump, none of them really like me ... Do they?

Her body shook as the void's chill bit harder.

Never mind that for now, Let's see if I can find an exit.

Sakura moved to start running, but froze.

You're at the top of a hill, silly! Do you want to fall and break your neck?

She looked down, finding more void extending below her feet. Cautiously, she reached down, expecting her fingers to thread themselves through blades of trodden grass. They descended further, until they were reaching below the soles of her shoes. Her arm went past her feet, then her head, then the rest of her body, until she was standing upright again.

Or is this downright?

Her brain did another double take, and her irritation grew.

"What the heck is going on here!?" she roared. She kicked the space in front of her, hoping for at least some physical, kickable object to receive her frustration. Instead, a few puffs of dirt flew off her runners and vanished into the void.

Annoyed, Sakura started to run. She went in what she thought was forward, and kept on going and going. With every minute she ran without meeting any wall or object, the voice in her head grew louder: *Weakling.*

She growled furiously and pressed on. The voice shouted louder, and she shrieked to push it back down. Her feet grew heavier and her breath scratched at her throat. She couldn't even fall to her knees, as her momentum carried her about an invisible pivot in space and she ended up back on her feet.

Her every joint ached as she panted. Her shirt, already covered with dirt and stains from weeks of training, grew damp, and clung to her body. That alone was enough to upset her. Throw in the panic-inducing landscape of nothingness about her, and she was utterly miserable.

"Hello," she screamed hoarsely. "Somebody, answer me! Help me, please!"

Not even an echo responded.

Her frustration and fear pushed her internal dam to breaking point, and tears started to trickle down her cheeks.

Why am I here? Because I asked Lee to train me. Is this another one of his schemes to get me to give up?

She voicelessly growled, "If it is, you win, Lee!"

The void simply stared back at her.

*Come to think of it, why did I even need training? I shouldn't even be here. I'm no magician. I'm just a girl from the gymnastics club. I listen to BabyMetal, Queen, and Kana Nishino ... Why did I even have to pick up that book in the first place? It was supposed to be a present for Naoko. If I hadn't opened the book, **she'd** be the one doing the magic. **She'd** be better for this job than me! She cosplays as Hermione Granger, for God's sake!*

The void encroached upon her, and she noticed the tears weighing down her cheeks. Her strident breathing stung at her throat as she sighed and wiped her face dry. Her aching muscles whined as she rose to her full height, and with all her strength willed a vision into her mind: the Cards, floating about her, and the words she heard them utter: *You are the master we want, Sakura.*

"No bother crying," she whispered to herself. "No matter what happens, I'll definitely be alright."

Suddenly, a flash of light erupted from her skin and swirled in the void about her. The cyclone of photons ripped the void apart and banished it to the furthest horizon, before assembling into the guise of a woman clothed in the most magnificent white raiment. Her black eyes gazed down at Sakura, and offered her the warmest smile.

Sakura stared flabbergasted at the vibrant wight, and murmured, "I got nothing."

"That's hardly true, Master," said the woman. "You had me the whole time, from the moment you opened the book, and had more than enough strength to bring me out."

Sakura looked about and saw the luminance around her. A thought struck her brain.

"You're the Light Card, aren't you?" she said.

"Correct," said the woman, her grin turning mischievous. "But here's the real prize-winning question: The Light, and what, are two sides of the same coin?"

Sakura pursed her lips. She pondered for a moment, a dopey, oblivious expression on her face, until her bewildered mind considered the void that had consumed her before.

"It's not Dark, is it?" she asked with a confused frown.

Suddenly, that very same inky blackness sped from the horizon toward her. It condensed into a woman identical to the Light Card, but with an inverted colour scheme. Her white eyes stared downward at Sakura, and gave her that same smile.

"When the carrier of the Light is ready, the Dark shall

come to test her," said the Dark.

"What?" said Sakura deadpanned. "*That* was just a test?"

"And there are more to come," said the Light with a chuckle.

"Oh, come on!" exclaimed Sakura. "I'm just a girl from the gymnastics club."

"Which is exactly why we chose you," said the Dark. "If we'd chosen someone with great power or aspirations, we'd have been consumed by their quest."

"But if we had someone with a kind heart, like you, our true essence could shine," said the Light.

The Light and Dark floated toward each other and joined hands.

"And now that you passed the test, it is time for us to begin our service under our new master," they said. Sakura stood a little dumbstruck by the sight, and started to shuffle under their expectant gazes. The Dark leaned forward and said, "You need to seal us now."

"Oh, right!" exclaimed Sakura. She summoned the Sealing Staff. "Return to thine intended forms, Clow Cards!"

A wave of gratitude and excitement flooded through the Cards' beings, which Sakura could feel as clearly as her own thoughts, as they began to dissolve into their inert forms. Yet, as the transformation neared completion, a twinge of sadness and fear flowed from them into Sakura's heart.

"What's the matter?" she asked.

"We do want you to be our master," said the Dark.

"But that, ultimately, is not for us to decide," said the Light.

Sakura frowned, "Then who decides? Me? Of course, I'll be your master."

"The one who decides," murmured the Light.

"The one whose duty it is to judge you," murmured the Dark.

The Cards wafted into her hands, and their voices echoed in her mind: "He is Yue."

* * *

Tomoyo blinked as if something had flown into her eye. In the space of that blink, two Cards had appeared in Sakura's hands. That didn't seem out of the ordinary; she'd had them on hand since she started training. What did seem weird was Sakura's expression.

"What's the matter, Sakura?" she asked.

Sakura snapped to attention, as if Tomoyo had snuck up on her, and she looked up from gazing at the Cards in her hand. She looked around and saw the landscape of Tokushima, bathed in mid-morning sunlight. She turned and saw Lee and Kero. Lee's grin was a very amused, intrigued expression to behold, while Kero's smile was absolutely ecstatic.

"Sakura got two new Cards!" he roared.

"Oh did you!" exclaimed Tomoyo delighted. Sakura showed them off, and Tomoyo read the name placards aloud, "The Light, The Dark. What do they do?"

"They're the two master Cards of the whole deck," said Kero. "The Dark is the head of Cards like Windy and Shadow. The Light, she's over Cards like Sword and Shield. With these, ya'll get even better at being Master of the Clow."

Sakura beamed, and thanked her friends for their support. Though it wasn't long before she had to console Tomoyo on being unable to film the whole experience.

"Maybe we could reshoot it with the cards' help?" asked Tomoyo hopefully.

"Snow ball's chance," said Sakura flatly.

Lee approached them and said, "Congratulations on passing another test, Cardcaptor."

Sakura pursed her lips suspiciously and said, "That wasn't your doing, was it?"

"Was what?" asked Lee.

"The Dark coming and grabbing me," asked Sakura.

"The Cards act when they want," replied Lee. He added with a smirk, "Until they find a new master."

Sakura grinned, "Well, they've got one now."

Lee shrugged, "Almost … But not yet."

* * *

Night fell, and the moon started to rise above the horizon. It was a full moon, and it blasted a blanket of pale light across the landscape. Sakura's wings reflected that light, and shimmered beautifully as she stood at the top-most part of the hill and awaited Lee's instructions.

"This will be your final test," said Lee, trying his best to ignore Tomoyo the Paparazza, who ogled Sakura through her digital camera. Kero sat on her head, trying hard not to look nervous.

"I am ready," said Sakura.

"You'd better be," said Lee. "You need to resonate with the Fly Card, and use that resonance as a conduit to funnel magical energy to the Card. That way, you will be able to fly for much longer, and a hell of a lot faster."

"Language," mumbled Sakura.

"Focus!" barked Lee. Sakura squeaked, but maintained her composure. She directed her energy to her shoulder blades, where her body met her wings. Every breath she drew filled her with light, which passed into the wings as she exhaled. She started to feel the ebb and flow of Fly's breathing, and adjusted her respiration to match. Fly matched her back.

Soul Resonance, said the voice in her mind.

Her eyes fluttered open, and she saw an amazed expression on Tomoyo's face, an excited one on Kero's, and an enthused one on Lee's. Why, she didn't know. But she could ask later.

"Now, Cardcaptor," said Lee. "Fly as high as you can." He pointed to his ear, supporting an earpiece with the Daidoujii logo. "I'll be in your ear the whole time."

Sakura nodded, and her wings started to flap. She ascended, her mind focused on nothing else but the climb. Her eyes gazed outward over the horizon, which started to curve as if bent toward her. The haze of the atmosphere turned to the tingly bite of ice crystals as she passed through a peppering of clouds. When she cleared them, she went on further.

Breathe in, she thought.

And out, thought Fly.

Her head felt like something was pulling it to the side, but she ignored it and kept her mind on the ascent. It pulled harder, until she could no longer keep her focus and she grabbed her head to steady herself. Suddenly, her every nerve screeched with information she'd theretofore blocked out. She was freezing, and her lungs burned with lack of air. She was so overcome with the sensory load she didn't realise for at least half a minute that she was falling.

That was when she started to scream.

"You're falling, aren't you?" said Lee into his microphone. He watched her barely visible form tumbling through the air.

"Sakura!" screamed Tomoyo.

Kero leapt into the air to fly toward her, but a hand gripped his tail and forced him to the ground.

"Stay down," hissed Lee as he tightened his grip on the Beast of the Seal.

"You tryin' to kill her," shouted Kero.

Lee ignored Kero's struggling and Tomoyo's panicked shrieks and spoke calmly into the microphone.

"Sakura, you are falling, but you still have the Sealing Staff in your hand," he said. "The Fly Card is still active. I can sense it. She's just waiting for you to re-establish the link."

Sakura flailed through the air, wincing as the clouds struck her like a floating bed of brambles. Only Lee's voice managed to reach her through her utterly freaked-out tumult, and the last vestige of her sanity held onto it like a lifeline.

"Regain your focus, Cardcaptor," said Lee. "Re-establish your link, just like you did with Light and Dark."

The image of the Light and Dark, two sides of the coin, hand in hand, entered her mind. She closed her eyes, and reached out through the telepathic gap. She couldn't find the conduit to Fly, but she kept searching.

Don't cry, she told herself. *No matter what happens, I'll definitely be alright.*

In the void, a hand caught her. Wings exploded from her back, and vectored into the wind. In a graceful manoeuvre, Sakura swooped, only nicking the top of the trees before veering into the sky. With a delightful shriek, she swerved about the valley, her speed greater than anything she'd ever experienced, even with Windy's help.

On the ground, Lee gave a proud guffaw. Tomoyo meanwhile was overjoyed to see her friend pull out of the dive and subsequently soar around the Tokushima Mountains.

"She did it!" she screeched, punching the air and dancing around in amazement.

Lee released Kero, who launched himself from the ground and shot straight after his master.

"Sakura!" he bellowed when he got within ear-reach of the speeding bird-girl.

"Kero! I did it!" exclaimed the girl.

"That's my Cardcaptor Sakura!" Kero shouted.

Sakura giggled ecstatically, and proceeded to fly a loop-the-loop, then a half Cuban Eight. Poor Kero, overwhelmed with shock – and holding a latent death grudge for Lee – couldn't keep up with the girl, whose joy could have fuelled Fly for the rest of the night.

On the ground, Tomoyo's nerves calmed and her grin slowly turned to a proud smile. She switched off her camcorder and looked over to Lee. The boy had a similarly proud grin, with only the slightest twinge of relief. Tomoyo could tell it wasn't for Sakura's surviving the test.

"You're glad she proved herself," she said. Lee heard her, but didn't respond. She went on, "You wanted her to succeed, and were afraid she wouldn't. Why?"

Lee looked at her and said, "You'll see soon enough." His eyes turned back to Sakura performing aerial manoeuvres, and shook his head incredulously.

The Clow Cards aren't toys, he thought with only half-hearted disapproval.

"If her training's done, we still have another week of school holidays left," said Tomoyo. "Mister Kinomoto will be getting worried soon."

Lee hummed at the thought, and then said, "It'll be done tomorrow." With a gleam directed to Tomoyo's camera, he added, "I have one more test to try."

* * *

Sakura stood before Lee, his hands held behind his back, as a drill sergeant would view a graduating cadet proudly. Sakura looked back at him, a smile riding on her lips. Nearby, Tomoyo filmed the entire exchange, and was glad that the morning light was so perfect as to capture Sakura's graduation.

"Your training is complete," proclaimed Lee. "To honour your completion, you will have your prize." With a flourish, he brandished her phone. The battery indicator was full. "I charged it last night, so you may now speak to Mister Tsukishiro."

Sakura beamed excitedly and took the phone. She momentarily recalled the times Lee had snatched the phone away, and eyed him suspiciously. He offered her a smile and said, "I hope he will be glad to hear from you."

Sakura grinned, and unlocked the phone to find the contacts app. Suddenly, it vanished from her hand, and was back in Lee's. He scratched his nose, as if he didn't realise he'd snatched the phone back. He looked to his hand incredulously.

"Here, I'm sure he'd love to hear your voice," he said, a

very slight snideness to his voice. Sakura took the phone back and resumed her search for Yukito's number. A strike as quick as lightning to her hand launched the phone into Lee's. In his free hand, he held his stick, pointed fixedly at Sakura. Amber eyes directed a fierce gaze into emerald eyes.

Sakura launched herself forward, lunging for the phone. Lee's palm hit her chest, and a gust of wind threw her head-over-heels. Tomoyo and Kero moved to help her, but met an invisible wall.

Kero saw hidden paper charms on trees all over the place and snapped, "Oi! Trainin's s'posed to be finished, right?"

Lee didn't answer. He sauntered over to Sakura, who pulled herself to her feet.

"Don't you want to talk to your dearest love?" he asked sardonically.

"You gonna let me?" barked a very fed-up Sakura.

"You gonna *make* me?" taunted Lee, twirling his stick about his hands.

Sakura huffed, and summoned the Sealing Staff. She struck the Sword Card, and with the blade in hand, she lunged. Lee darted aside, avoiding her strokes and swipes. He swatted the blade aside with his stick and swivelled to strike her head. She leaned back to avoid the swipe, and gave a roundhouse kick aimed for Lee's head.

Lee stumbled backward, though his smirk remained as he steadied himself and waited for her next attack. He deflected a swipe to the right, and she parried to her left, before swivelling to bring the blade along a horizontal path. Lee threw the phone into the air to free his other hand, and with it he threw up his magical barrier. A wave of surprise and fear hit him as the barrier didn't block the blow, but merely deflected it. Thinking quickly, he somersaulted over the path of the blade and stumbled against a tree.

Sakura saw the phone falling through the air, Yukito's

number still visible on the screen. She reached for it greedily.

Lee's hand beat her to it. She saw his thoroughly evil smile and fumed. She deactivated Sword, and cast out Shadow. A barrage of umbral blades charged Lee, but melted away when he summoned his lightning spell.

But Shadow had served his purpose as a distraction.

Sakura swatted the Sealing Staff against Lee's head, and then knocked the phone of his hands. She reached to catch it again.

"*Fēnghuá!*" Lee shouted. A gust of wind caught the phone and carried it into a nook on a tree further down the hill. Sakura wasted no time, her eyes fixated upon her prize, and summoned the Jump Card. And as she bounded up the height of the nearest tree, Lee watched her with the giddiest smile. He scooped up his stick and sprinted up the tree into which the phone had fallen, and landed on a branch right in front of Sakura. He threw her a cocky look, which she resolutely matched.

"Mirror!" she cried. Lee's heart skipped beats as the Card formed effigy of his opponent, mirroring her confident expression. Sakura charged him with the Sealing Staff, parrying his blows while delivering her own. The Mirror used her fists, and Lee had to block both their strikes. Sakura came from the right, her Sealing Staff's beak locked around his ankle. She threw him off balance, but hadn't expected him to take advantage of it, and he used it to deliver a swift kick to Mirror's chest. The doppelganger fell from the branch and deactivated mid-fall.

Lee recovered his footing and turned to see Sakura similarly falling from the branch. In a brief fit of alarm, he lunged to catch her, but grabbed thin air. The image of Sakura vanished, to his surprise, in a flurry of fractal colours. He quickly jerked his head to see the real Sakura charging for the phone. She managed to reach the nook, only in time to nudge the phone out of its holding place. Lee grabbed her ankle and yanked her away from the phone, and it fell toward the ground.

Sakura leapt down to a lower branch just in time to catch the phone, but was still frustrated by Lee, who'd lodged his feet in a fork in the branch just above. With his stick, he proceeded to swat the phone out of her hands, or lever her fingers apart when she caught it. His laughter was infectious, as Sakura started to giggle at the fun of their struggle. Eventually, Sakura lost her hold, and the phone fell. Lee unhooked his feet and launched himself downward. He caught the phone just before it hit the ground and he rolled to break his fall. Sakura appeared behind him with wings on her feet, and swung her Sealing Staff to knock the phone out of his hands once more.

They exchanged blow after blow with stick and fist, while engaging in a game of hacky-sack with the phone. Sakura swerved to avoid a head blow from Lee's stick and caught it on the ground with her foot. Lee's impulse to pull upward gave her a jolt of momentum as she soared over his head, caught the phone mid-air, and landed behind him.

The Shield Card activated, just in time to meet Lee's magic-fuelled punch.

When the dust and smoke cleared, there stood Sakura, safe behind Shield, which had withstood the magician's attack. The phone was in her hand – a triumphant feeling, to say the least.

Completely out-of-breath, Lee rose to his feet, the pain in his knuckles nothing compared to the pride that filled him. He only smiled, and bowed to his victorious opponent.

Sakura still regarded him warily, but let her eyes turn to the phone. She hit 'call' and waited for the it to connect.

"Sakura?" came Yukito's heavenly voice.

"Hi, Yukito," said Sakura cheerily.

"Has hiking been difficult? You're panting," he said.

"Oh yeah, hiking has been *really* tough," she said, her glare directed at Lee. "But really fun as well."

"When will you be getting back?"

"We're going to head back today, should get back by tonight," said Sakura.

"That's good," exclaimed Yukito. "There's an *ennichi* festival on tomorrow night. Touya and I were going to go. You're welcome to come along too."

Sakura giggled with excitement. "I'd love to go. Can Tomoyo come?"

"Oh, of course. The more, the merrier!"

At that moment, Sakura had an epiphany. She pressed the phone to her chest and looked over her shoulder.

"Lee?" she asked in English. "Do you, by chance, like ennichi festivals?"

11 | Modern-Yaki

Lee's on-call driver took them straight back to Takamatsu, a trip *much* shorter than their hike a few weeks earlier. Before taking them to the airport, Lee decided to stop by a bathhouse so that Sakura and Tomoyo could wash off their weeks of dirt and fatigue. Kero was plenty grateful for that, not so much for the head-slap he earned for commenting on Sakura's body odour.

During the trip back, Sakura and Tomoyo prepared the story of their long camping trip in Tokushima. Sakura needed to avoid any mention of magic, rigorous training, or nearly plummeting to her death. Luckily, they didn't need to come up with an alibi for Sakura's many bruises and scratches, as Lee's healing magic handled them just fine.

When they arrived at Tokyo Haneda, Sakura felt a little disappointed to see Lee go.

Why would I be? she asked herself. *He's still a meanie, and a bit of a bully too.*

Tomoyo could read her thoughts as if they were a bright neon sign on her face, and snickered at her friend's expression.

When Sakura reached her house, Franklin assaulted her with a flurry of hugs and chidings about being away so long. She and Tomoyo told their story, which for the most part was true: they'd gone camping in Tokushima, hiked around for a few weeks, and even filmed some footage for their next video. When they were finally done with the story, it was well into the night.

The following day, Sakura went to Tomoyo's house to look at the videos of their trip. Much to Sakura's dismay (though hardly to her surprise), most of the shots were captured without her knowledge, at times that were not her most proud moments.

Several involved Sakura falling and scraping a knee or elbow, others showed her many face-plants into the dirt, with her backside up in the air. But, as the clips progressed, they grew more interesting, and even playful, as they chronicled Lee's games with cat-and-mouse.

Then, after the photos of Sakura and Lee chatting amiably (which made Tomoyo chuckle and Kero fume), there was a night time shot. Sakura stood at the top of the hill that had been their home, and diligently listened to Lee's instructions. The clip elicited memories of Sakura's resonance with Fly, and made her heart race with elation. Her brow furrowed, however, when her recorded self established the resonance.

"Wow, my eyes were glowing," she said, a tad perturbed.

"That's the resonance workin'," said Kero.

"It's creepy," said Sakura.

"It's awesome," said a grinning Tomoyo. "Oh, this video is going to be so popular when I upload it."

That made Sakura shudder, though she didn't know if it was shame or trepidation.

However, after all the scrapes, bruises, blows, games of hide-and-seek, and of course the brush with death, what really grabbed Sakura's interest was her final test. As she scrambled for her phone, the video captured something that she never thought she'd see: Lee was smiling, as if he was having *fun*.

"He's actually kinda cute when he smiles," she thought aloud.

Kero suddenly burst into her field of view, his face crumpled into an expression of fury.

"Oi! Don't be fallin' for that brat, ya hear!" he bellowed.

Sakura could only stammer, "What? I wasn't –"

"Snow Rabbit Yukito is the dude ya like, right?!" snapped Kero. He thrust his plush-toy finger in her face. "RIGHT!?"

"Of course, he is," exclaimed Sakura. "He's my Number One! I was just saying …"

"Sayin' what? Spit it out!" growled Kero.

"It's just nice that Lee isn't all mean," said Sakura. "I'm glad that he's started being nice to me, is all. I hope that he'll be my friend."

Kero glared at her a moment longer, until he finally swivelled and said, "Well then, friend-zone is good. Friend-zone the brat."

Beast of the Seal floated downward to the coffee table and proceeded to load his teacup with sugar. Sakura was dumbstruck, but Tomoyo wasn't so taken aback – in fact, she found it hilarious. She held back her laughter long enough to ask, "Kero, you seem to have a grudge against Lee."

"He's a dumb brat," spat Kero as he refilled his cup.

"It seems more than that," said Sakura. "What did he do to you?"

"It's what *he* did to *you*!" said Kero. "Bullyin' ya, hittin' ya, callin' ya names, shoutin' how weak ya are! An' then ya turn around and say, 'Awww! Ain't he cute.'"

"Well, we've made up," Sakura insisted. "He's trained me, and he encouraged me. The video shows that he's at least lightened up a little. Plus," – she thought back to all her bad moods – "I don't like holding grudges."

"An' he tells me I made a bad choice for the new Clow Master," snapped Kero, clearly oblivious to anything she'd said. "What idiot tells me I pick a bad candidate? I'm Kerberus the Selector, *lan yeung!*"

Kero proceeded to curse and growl in Cantonese, before finally shooting into the air and yelling, "An' he almost killed ya with that stunt with Fly! He stopped me from helpin' ya too!" He turned to Sakura, tears dribbling down his face, and threw his arms as far around her neck as he could reach. "You're the best, Sakura," he sobbed. "After losin' Clow, I couldn't take it if I lost another master as awesome as you."

Sakura giggled at the complement, and patted her friend on his furry back. She eyed the Book of Clow on the table, the Cards glowing softly within. She could feel their sensations through their resonating link, and gave a warm smile.

"I know I complain a lot," she said. "But to be honest, I'm so glad I met all of you. And it's been so fun collecting you all and making these videos."

"Amen to that," said Tomoyo with a raise of her glass.

"And now that I've proven I can be a good Clow Master, maybe Lee and I can be friends," said Sakura. "So, maybe you and Lee can bury the hatchet?"

Kero suddenly flew away from Sakura's chest and snapped, "Never! A cool guy like me will never be friends with that *lan yeung!*"

Sakura frowned, "What does that mean?"

Tomoyo whipped out her phone for a translation. A few seconds later, her eyes darkened and she said, "You don't want to know."

* * *

The skies above were a hazy dark blue, with only the faintest hints of fading red the sun left behind. The lamps lining the pathway, along with the bright stall signs, imbued those navy skies with a soft yellow glow. Sakura stood at the entrance to the Tsukimine Shrine, Kero playing dead on her shoulder, Tomoyo to her left, and three weeks worth of allowance in her pocket.

Touya stood behind her, his hands in his pockets and his face a bored mug.

"Don't be goin' too far away," he said.

"Oh please, once I get my takoyaki, I'm not going anywhere!" bellowed Sakura. Touya saw the plush toy on his sister's shoulder, and pursed his lips. Yukito stood beside him and chuckled, "Make sure you get some for me too."

"Will do, Mister Tsukishiro!" said Tomoyo.

Sakura fixed her eyes on the festival and exclaimed, "Let us feast!"

She charged for the first takoyaki stall she could find, and ordered two servings – one with hoisin and the other with chilli. Tomoyo stealthily pinched an empty box, into which Sakura dropped two of each.

"This is your share, Kero," she said as she surreptitiously handed her plush toy friend the box. Kero grinned excitedly, nabbed the box and scooted through the air and into a nearby bush. As the two girls gazed after him, Tomoyo murmured, "A thousand yen says he'll be demanding okonomiyaki[15] in less than five minutes."

"No bet," said Sakura flatly.

Sure enough, hardly a minute after the girls sat to enjoy their treats did Kero's voice hiss in Sakura's mind, "More takoyaki!"

"Kero?" mumbled a surprised Sakura. She and Tomoyo looked around but he wasn't there.

"I'm not there, I'm resonating with you," said Kero's voice in her mind. "Since you're getting better with magic, I can do this. Now, more takoyaki!"

Sakura cringed at the idea of being psychically assaulted by Kero's insatiable appetite.

Mental note, she thought. *Ask Lee to teach me how to block telepathy.*

---

15   A savoury crepe originating from the Kansai and Hiroshima areas, popular throughout Japan.

Touya sat down with four boxes of takoyaki and yakisoba[16], Yukito holding another four. Tomoyo's eyes bugged out at the sight.

"Do older boys really have such an appetite?" she whispered to Sakura.

"Nope, just Yukito," said Sakura. The girls watched as Yukito ripped through seven boxes of food in the time it took Touya to eat just half of one. He tossed his last box in the bin and sighed, "Ah, delicious!" Then he noticed Sakura and Tomoyo, wide eyed with surprise. A red hue rode on his cheeks as he said, "Is it that strange?"

"Not at all," exclaimed Sakura. "It's a sign of a healthy body if you can eat that much."

A voice riddled with concern sounded, "Really? I was going to ask if he had a thyroid problem."

The four looked up and saw Lee, half a taiyaki[17] fish cake in his hand. Touya suddenly launched to his feet and growled, "Get lost, creep!"

"Touya, it's alright!" said Sakura as she caught his wrist. "Lee's not going to attack me or anything."

"What? You're all chatty now?" snapped Touya. "Didn't this little creep beat you up?"

Sakura stammered, her eyes darting between a furious Touya and Lee, nonchalantly nibbling away at his taiyaki. Thankfully, Tomoyo was better at thinking on her feet.

"He was auditioning," she said.

"Auditioning?" asked Yukito.

"We were thinking of a rival for our Cardcaptor Sakura character, right?" said Tomoyo, her eyes fixated on Sakura. "We figured we could have a boy who's also hunting the Cards." She looked at Lee and said, "Right?"

Lee shrugged, "Sure. I guess I got a little too into the character." To Touya, he said, "Sorry about the kick to the head."

Touya advanced furiously, but Sakura put herself right

---

16   Japanese-style fried noodle.
17   A fish-shaped cake, often filled with sweet bean paste.

between the two.

"Lee's a friend," she insisted. "I invited him along. So be nice to him."

Touya's lips pursed tightly as he glared Lee down. The boy just smiled right back at him, his eyes yelling, "Come at me, bro!" But Touya knew better than to start a fight with a whole lot of people around. That, and he could see Nadeshiko standing beside a nearby tree, her wide eyes silently begging, "Be nice."

"I ain't buyin' anything for him," he said.

"That's fine, Mister Touya," said Lee. "I got a wad of cash before I came. Maybe I can treat you?"

Touya could have bashed the kid senseless right then and there, were it not for Yukito's hand on his shoulder. The pale-faced boy said, "Oh, could I have another serving of yakisoba?"

Lee raised an eyebrow and said, "You really should get a diabetes test done."

He did buy some more food for everyone, including Touya, who took it begrudgingly. They ate as they walked, Touya's burning stare fixed on the boy who seemed far too friendly with Sakura.

"He isn't attacking her, and Sakura seems comfortable around him," said Yukito.

"That ain't it," said Touya.

"Then what?" asked Yukito after swallowing another heavy mouthful of noodles.

"I just don't like the creep," grumbled Touya. "And I don't like that Sakura's all chummy with him. She should only spend time with nice guys."

Touya expected a reply, and when none came, he turned to see Yukito pretending to talk on the phone. His friend suddenly held out the mimed phone and said, "Touya, it's Doctor Freud. He really wants to discuss your sister complex."

Touya pushed his friend away with a mumble of, "Shaddup!"

Sakura, meanwhile, was trying to carry on a conversation with Lee and Tomoyo. But a particular voice, whispering in a Kansai accent, refused to let up inside her head.

Modern-Yaki! Modern-Yaki! Modern-Yaki! Modern-Yaki! Modern-Yaki! Modern-Yaki! Modern-Yaki! Modern-Yaki!

"It was so Modern-Yaki[18] how I managed to Modern-Yaki that Modern-Yaki," said Sakura. That earned quite a shocked expression from Tomoyo, and a chuckle from Lee.

"Kerberus is harassing you, right?" he asked.

"Gah, how do I block out his telepathy?" she snapped.

"That'd take a bit of practice," said Lee. "For now, do what you must to shut him up."

Sakura scanned around for an okonomiyaki stall, and bolted toward one next to a goldfish scooping game. As she ran off, Tomoyo noted Lee's eyes fixated on her. Her curiosity started to bubble.

"You didn't answer me before," she said. "Why were you so afraid she wouldn't succeed?"

"I hope she has enough money to pay for all that food," said Lee as if he'd not heard the question.

"Stop dodging," said Tomoyo. "When we first met you, I was too afraid to notice. But I did start to see it. That face you have when you look at her – I see that face all the time."

Lee finally looked at her, a well-practiced sense of control allowing only the lightest tinge of red below his eyes.

"Where do you see it?" he asked.

"Mostly whenever Sakura sees Mister Tsukishiro," said Tomoyo with a smile. That made Lee's lips tighten irately, which only made Tomoyo's smile grow wider. "Someone's

---

18   A style of okonomiyaki in which toppings of noodles are added. The actual word is *modanyaki*, which is a contraction of *mori dakusan okonomiyaki*, meaning "crepe piled high." But it is most often rendered as <u>*modern-yaki*</u> in English.

jealous," she giggled. "What? Was it love at first sight, just like with her and Tsukishiro? I remember how you looked when he came to help us in the alley that day. You had the most scared look."

"I saw how she looked at him," said Lee. "For the first time in my life, I actually froze."

"Well, what I don't understand is how you could attack her like that if you fell in love with her so fast," Tomoyo wondered. "It's like: fall in love one second, and then fighting the next."

Lee sighed, "It wasn't in a second." Tomoyo frowned. Lee went on, "The Lee Clan boasts some of the most skilled fortune tellers in the world. My mother is one of them, and foresaw the coming of the new Clow Master before I was born. She knew where it would be and when, but never who. Sakura hadn't been identified until about two months before she found the Book of Clow."

He took out his phone, and showed Tomoyo a photo taken from Sakura's gymnastics meet the previous year. She was smiling brightly, a baton in one hand, and a second place medal in the other.

"It was like I'd been struck by lightning," said Lee. "I saw this picture, and I had to meet her. I demanded that I be allowed to observe her in Japan – I'd never demanded something like that before. My father almost tanned me. But he let me go, so I could meet the one chosen by Clow."

Tomoyo gripped her mouth tightly to restrain the joyous screeches that threatened to burst from her.

Oh my God, this is so sweet and cool and awesome! This is so totally going in a video! Oh my God! I should have filmed this whole thing!

Lee turned to her and withdrew in alarm when he saw her blood-red face of restraint. She quickly calmed herself before squeaking, "Don't mind me."

Lee coughed slightly and said, "Anyway, you have your answer. I want her to succeed and become the new

Master."

Neither of them noticed Sakura approaching, and Lee jumped three feet in the air when she said, "I'm glad you feel that way, Lee."

"How long were you listening?" he exclaimed breathlessly.

Sakura smiled warmly and said, "Enough to hear you say you want me to succeed."

Behind them, Tomoyo laughed her head off. Sakura managed to ignore her, and kept her emerald gaze locked on Lee's amber eyes.

"That makes me really happy that you support me," she said. "Thanks so much."

"You're welcome," said Lee.

Sakura sighed and said, "Now, if you don't mind, I've got an annoying Beast of the Seal to feed." As she hopped away, she grumbled, "Yes, I'm on my way. Jeez!"

Lee turned to Tomoyo and said, "Miss Daidouji, I think you're enjoying this *way* more than you should."

Tomoyo only laughed evilly in reply.

* * *

A little-travelled path, adjacent to the main alley of stalls and shops, led onto a lookout over the festival. There, Kero wolfed down all the takoyaki Sakura had given him. He hadn't started pestering Sakura straight away. Instead, he'd taken money he'd stolen from her pocket ahead of time, and stealthily dropped it into the moneyboxes of a dozen different stalls before pinching servings of food when no one was looking.

Much to his chagrin, none of the boxes had contained that which he craved.

"I doth verily decree, I must haveth of the Modern-Yaki!" he proclaimed, confusing people within ear reach of the lookout.

Thus began Kero's half-hour-long psychic harassing of his master, demanding his favourite food, until said master appeared bearing five boxes of Modern-style okonomiyaki. He floated toward her with a joyous expression, as if he were running through a field of wild flowers to his dearest love.

Before he could grab the first box, Sakura yanked it out of his reach and snapped, "Bother me like that again, and you'll never eat again."

"Hey, you only gave me four takoyaki! I was hungry!" retorted Kero.

"Oh yeah? What's that other pile of boxes there?" asked Sakura.

"I was hungry!" insisted Kero.

"Promise me you'll never bug me like that again," said Sakura. "In fact, apologise for it, *then* promise you'll never do it again."

"Fine then, I'm sorry," rasped Kero. "Now, give me my Modern-Yaki!"

Sakura withheld the boxes with raised eyebrows. Kero met her gaze unwaveringly and defiantly.

"Okay, if you're not going to apologize," Sakura began. She strutted to the edge of the lookout, and held the boxes out over the railing.

Kero folded his arms with a scoff. "You wouldn't dare!" Sakura feinted, and instantly Kero collapsed into a fretting child. "I'm sorry, my dearest lord of all lordy lords, Sakura the Magnificently All-beautiful Goddess! I will never pester you again! Please, may I have the Modern-Yaki! Please, please, please, please, pretty please with a chocolate liqueur cherry on top."

Sakura glanced down at the floating teddy bear with a smirk. It felt amazing to see Kero to grovel before her like that. She took pity on him, and placed the boxes before the desperate wretch. In the next second, the creature ripped open the first box and literally belly-flopped into the food.

"I left Tomoyo, Lee, Touya, and Yukito at the festival, so I'm going to head back," she said.

"Roger!" exclaimed Kero through a mouthful of okonomiyaki. He kept chewing, but stopped and hesitated. "Lee, you said?" He turned, an irate glimmer in his eye, and growled, "The brat is here?"

"I invited him, remember?" replied Sakura.

"I thought you were kiddin'," snapped Kero.

"No, I was being nice," said Sakura. "I want to be friends with him. And he's started being really nice too. In fact, he just told me he really wants me to be the new Clow Master."

The Beast of the Seal harrumphed, "He's still a brat. You fall for him and I'll deck you!"

Sakura glared at Kero through narrowed eyelids and murmured, "Enjoy the food I bought you." She turned and stepped down the path. She would have continued to marvel at her friend's glutinous personality, but Lee's words of approval were still fresh in her mind.

I want her to succeed and become the new master, he had said.

An image of Light and Dark flashed through her mind, along with their voices making the same statement. But there was something they said that Lee hadn't. Sakura quickly turned around, spurred by curiosity, and raced back up to the lookout. Kero was still there, sucking a cardboard box dry of the okonomiyaki sauce.

"Kero, who's Yue?" she asked.

The box almost flew down Kero's gullet as he gasped in shock. One long bout of coughing and spluttering later, Kero turned and said, "Yue? Got no idea."

"Oh yeah?" asked Sakura sardonically. "Mighty shocked reaction for someone who doesn't know someone."

Kero stammered, "I ... uh ... Got nothin' ... umm ... ya know what, I thought you'd said 'Choowey' ... Yeah, it's how some people say 'Chewie,' ya know, from Star Wars ... Ya, me 'n' Mayhew go back a long way ... He owes me money, ya know. He bet me they'd never make Star Wars Seven, and what happens, eh?"

Sakura glared at the perspiring airborne creature, and her eyes narrowed. She said, "What are you hiding from me, Kerberus?"

Kero mewled nervously, and could not keep eye contact with his master. He kept silent, but his trembling only grew worse under her gaze.

I wonder if this telepathy goes both ways, said Sakura's voice in his head. His ears twitched, and he backed away.

"Stay outta my head, Kinomoto," snapped Kero. "There's some secrets that you really shouldn't know about."

Sakura drew near to him, and unleashed the Sealing Staff. She took Windy and Fly from her pocket and said, "You won't escape me, Kerberus. You said that it wasn't Lee's duty to judge me. The Light and Dark said that duty belongs to Yue." She got right in his face. "I've been through a lot for you and the Cards. And I have a right to know what else is coming. So tell me ... Who is Yue?"

Kero glared back at her, ready to bear his fangs like an animal cornered. His nerves neared to explosive levels, and his teeth were grit so tight they almost shattered.

Out went lights across the shrine. A gasp rippled through the crowd, followed by a flashing of phone lights. Those lights vanished soon after in a puff of smoke and a shriek.

Sakura glanced around nervously.

"Did you do this?" she asked.

"It ain't me," replied Kero.

Both of them felt weak in the knees, and their stomachs lurched. A sensation coursed through their bodies, familiar and yet overpowering. Mixed in with that feeling was a sickening scent completely alien to Sakura's mental nose. Her skin broke out in goosebumps at the oily, invading feeling piercing her mind. Within the presence, fuelled by multiple Clow Cards, she smelled malice, villainy, and an insatiable thirst for chaos.

She dragged herself to her feet, and looked up to see

the figure floating in the sky, girdled by orbs of red, brown, and yellow light. She was a sinister girl in a pointed leather hat and a flowing black dress, a serpent staff in her hand, and a malevolent grin on her face.

"*Dopyuu!*" gurgled the floating menace. "We meet at latht, Cardcaptor Thakuwa. *Dopyuu-hu-hu-hu!*"

"Sakura, those orbs are Clow Cards!" exclaimed Kero. "She's the other Cardcaptor!"

"Yeah, I got that," said Sakura, her staff raised. "But there's another sensation, and it makes me feel like I've eaten a dead rat. What is she? Something tells me she's not human."

Kero wafted into the air beside her and said, "She's a monster of destruction, sworn to ruin … what you'd call a Witch."

12 | Alice Axilotl

The Witch's purple tongue flicked hungrily, and she gurgled, *"Krudisu! Ez ubagda aktegri!"*[19] Her eyes flashed green as the yellow orb burst forth in a barrage of lightning bolts. Electricity ripped through the foliage around Sakura, setting them on fire. Sakura quickly soared into the air.

"Shield!" she shrieked, and her staff emitted her life-saving force field. The Witch's onslaught made Lee's blasts feel like a pillow fight. The strike threw her off balance, and she fell back into the blaze. She tumbled over charred wood and fire that singed her clothes.

"Sakura! We gotta get away from here!" exclaimed Kero. His tiny hands yanked her to her feet and she sprinted through the fire. The smoke stung her eyes and her lungs burned. She drew Windy from her pocket, and blasted the smoke away. With a quick moment to breathe, she saw the fire quickly spread across the shrine, haloing a rabble of frightened people.

Sakura cast out Watery, "Snuff these fires!"

Watery obediently launched himself from the staff, and swirled across the blaze. The air turned into a maelstrom of steam and ash, but it seemed to be working.

---

19   See Appendix on the Witchese Language.

"Sakura, watch out!" screamed Kero.

The Witch flew toward her, the yellow orb obeying the swing of her staff. A pulse of lightning ripped through Watery, who writhed and twitched in the air. Its agony translated through the resonance, and tore through Sakura's mind. She went rigid and couldn't scream. Watery severed the link and Sakura fell to the ground paralysed.

Kero frantically pulled at her hair and ears to wake her. She managed to gather her senses long enough to see the Witch, zooming down the paved path toward her. She tried to move but couldn't.

Shield! I need to raise Shield! I need to get Windy to do something! Why aren't I doing anything?

The Witch got close enough that Sakura could see her scaly skin and the murderous glare in her eyes.

Do something!

A shoe embedded itself in the Witch's face, and shot her right back down the path. Sakura looked up and saw Lee.

"Get up, now!" he barked. Sakura tried to push off the ground, but her arms were asleep. Lee grabbed her under the arm and lifted her to her feet. "Focus, Cardcaptor. You felt Watery's pain, but it didn't harm you. Focus on your own body!"

Sakura steadied her breathing, and imagined that her breath was a light that illuminated every part of her body.

You're alright, she told herself.

When she could stand on her own, she asked, "Where're the others?"

"Daidouji is with your brother and Tsukishiro," said Lee. "They're trying to get everyone out of the shrine as quickly as possible."

Sakura sighed with relief, and her eyes turned to the moaning Witch on the ground nearby. "Is this Yue?" she asked.

"Yue ain't no Witch," said Kero. "Nah, this is somethin' way more annoyin'."

The Witch pulled herself to her feet and picked up her serpent staff. A shoe-tread-shaped bruise covered most of her face, and her nose leaked like a faucet. Despite the injury, she still directed a healthy glare of malice at Lee.

"It'th been thoo wong, Coyote," she spat.

"Alice Axolotl, you've come a long way from ripping off third-rate sorcerers with plastic wands," returned Lee.

"Oi, Brat! You know this chick?" snapped Kero.

"A long time ago," said Lee. "You've been on the Reaper's list for years. I thought you'd made someone a Death Scythe by now."

"Oh well, *dopyuu*, a thawamander jutht wegwows a cut off weg," said Alice.

"They don't usually like snakes," said Lee, eying the serpent staff. "Someone's had help."

"None o' your beeth-waxth!" shouted Alice. She raised her staff, and the three orbs reappeared. The red orb merged with the staff. "*Tuagisu! Ubghakt akloetu!*" A searing beam shot from the mouth of the serpent staff, toward Lee. He threw out a paper charm and bellowed, "*Chèxiāo!*" But the beam didn't stop. Panicked, Lee raised his magic shield, and Sakura threw out her own. The force of the blast launched them over the treetops and into the street outside Tsukimine Shrine. A flood of terrified people almost trampled them as they fled the festival-turned-nightmare.

Alice soared over the trees and landed before them, the crowd withdrawing from her as if she were a disease. Lee and Sakura shot to their feet to confront the monster. Alice unleashed another fiery beam at Lee. This time, he was prepared, and focused his defences to envelop both Sakura and himself.

Meanwhile, Kero saw the mortified and confused expressions on every face in the crowd. He felt very exposed when he saw the astonished gazes directed at him.

"Sakura, we need some cover," he snapped.

Sakura threw out a Card, "Hide our guises, Illusion!"

She struck the Card, which enveloped them in its fractal patterns before going outward to infect every mind in the crowd. Instantly, the people backed away, blank-faced. Sakura then struck the Shadow, Wood, and Windy Cards, and an army of vines, dark tentacles, and gusts of wind caught every onlooker and carried them clear of the shrine.

When the bystanders were clear, Lee focused his energy into his magical shield, and turned Alice's beam back on her. The blast knocked her off balance, and Lee took his chance. He charged Alice, aiming a punch for her face. She dodged and swung her serpent staff. He blocked it with his forearm and delivered a knee to her stomach. Winded, Alice stumbled backwards and vomited brown translucent ooze.

With a sneer, Lee proclaimed, "I'm going to enjoy this a lot more than I should."

He raised his clenched fists and brought them down on her head. They made contact with a deafening thud, but Alice did not fall. She was as still as a statue. Then Lee and Sakura heard her murmur, *"Blikisu! Raz dziadazk!"* Her entire body simmered with dark brown light, and she rose to her feet. Annoyed, Lee threw a punch.

"Brat! Stop!" exclaimed Kero.

Alice stopped the blow with her finger. She then gripped his arm, twisted it with enough force to snap the bone, and then kicked Lee into a lamppost by the road.

Sakura gave a horrified shriek as her friend fell to the ground. She raced to help him, only to feel a sharp kick to her stomach that threw her across the road. Alice marched across the asphalt, swatting Kero out of the way, and ripped Sakura's backpack open with a mere flick of her wrist. What she saw inside made her salivate almost lasciviously.

"The Book of Cwow! At wast!" she exclaimed. She took the elegant book, hardly concerning herself with Sakura's flailing attempts to stop her. She looked down at the sobbing girl and said, "With thith, I'm now the Cwow

Mathter! The Cwow Cards awe mine!"

Bang!

A heavy rock smashed into Alice's head. The brown light still permeated her body, so it hardly left a mark. She turned to see a black haired girl, sporting a few bruises from being knocked around in the rush to escape. Beside her stood two tall boys.

"Tomoyo! Touya! Yukito!" exclaimed Sakura.

Touya stepped forward, another rock in his hand, and he roared, "Get away from her, you bitch!"

Alice snarled and raised her staff. Touya threw his rock, narrowly missing the Witch before she unleashed her fiery blast. Touya flew backward into Yukito, and they both hit the wall. Yukito was dazed, while Touya was out cold. Alice marched toward them, her serpent staff raised. She unleashed another blast squarely at the two boys, striking the Shield Card Sakura narrowly cast around her friends.

"Run!" she screamed. Dazed, Yukito lifted Touya, and Tomoyo shouldered them away.

Alice ceased her fire and swivelled to strike Sakura down, but the girl was already in motion. She tackled the Witch, and knocked the book out of her hand. She reached for it, but Alice grabbed her by the neck and threw her aside. Still in mid-air, Sakura cast Windy, who grabbed the book and launched it into the air. When Alice reached for it again, Sakura cast Wood, whose vines caught the Witch and held her down.

With a roar, Alice ripped the vines off her, and leapt after the book. Sakura swooped in and caught the book at the last minute. She hung above the asphalt like an angel of triumph, and she proclaimed, "I am the Master of the Clow. The Cards are my friends. You wanna mess with us, and you'll get curb-stomped!"

Alice flew after Sakura, frustration and fury burning in her eyes. The red orb burst from her serpent staff.

Sakura had an epiphany.

Alice was controlling the Illusion Card when I sealed it. That must mean my wand takes precedence over hers! So, if I treat this like any other Clow Card …

Sakura cast two Cards, "Snuff this fire and bind it! Windy! Watery!"

Windy and Watery flew out toward the front of Alice's blast, twirling about each other and merging. They struck the fiery wavefront and exploded in a vibrant flash and a writhing cloud of vapour. When the curtain of steam cleared, a horrible, rage-filled monstrosity of fire twitched and thrashed in Windy's chains. With a victorious grin, Sakura yelled, "Return to thine intended form, Clow Card!"

The flame beast dissolved into a Card, its deep masculine voice full of appreciation as it echoed in her mind, "I am free. Now, let me help you defeat this evil thing."

Alice was furious, and she screamed, "You damn –"

Bang!

The ball of flame smacked Alice good and hard, throwing her across the road. Sakura stepped back in shock, and glanced to the fire's shooter: Kero floated in the air, his eyes glowing bright red.

"Kero! How did you do that?" exclaimed Sakura.

"Now that you got the Fiery Card, I'ma gettin' my powers back," said the Beast of the Seal. "Now, if you can get the Earth Card off her, I can take my true form!"

With a cocky grin, Sakura turned to Alice, who pulled herself to her feet and shot a death glare at her. The Witch's mind was completely at the mercy of her fury. The yellow orb merged with her staff and she roared, "*Khatezo!*"

A bolt of lightning burst from the staff. Sakura cast out Shield. Kero pressed himself to her back to transfer as much of his magical power to her as he could, and the barrier held.

Alice ceased her firing and charged. She lunged for the book, but Sakura darted aside. The Witch didn't let up, and brought her staff down on Sakura's head. Though Sakura managed to block the blow, it sent her into the ground. She quickly recovered, summoned the Sword Card, and countered Alice's aerial strike. When the Witch reached for the book again, Sakura flicked it into the air and distracted the Witch with swipes and jabs of her blade, all the while playing hacky sack with the book.

Kero played interference, blasting the Witch with fireballs from his mouth. His shots weren't as lucky as his first, but it was enough to keep the Witch distracted. Sakura swatted her staff out of the way, and delivered a kick to her stomach. Alice stumbled backward, stunned, while Sakura passed the Book of Clow to Kero.

"Keep it away from her!" she commanded.

"Got it!" replied Kero, who promptly flew into the air and out of sight.

Now, it was just Sakura and Alice. The Witch summoned the brown orb into her body, and charged. She brought her staff down on Sakura's head, but missed and cracked the asphalt instead. Sakura swivelled to kick Alice's head, but met a face harder than rock. The Witch promptly grabbed her ankle and threw her into the ground like a ragdoll. The serpent staff came down a second time. Sakura cast the Jump Card and darted out of the way. She ignored the pain in her ankle and focused on the enemy.

Her strength ... that's probably the Earth Card Kero mentioned. How do I beat that?

She scrambled out of the path of another electrical blast.

What beats Earth? Rocks are hard and don't break easily. Wait! How many times have you tripped on a tree root that's sticking out of the ground?

She leapt through the air and landed gracefully, two Cards in her hand.

"Sap the earth from which ye draw thy strength! Wood! Flower!"

A forest of flowering plants erupted from the concrete in front of Alice, wrapping around her arms, legs, and throat. At Sakura's mental command, they yanked the brown light out of the Witch's body, holding another wailing entity in their grasp.

"Return to thine intended form, Clow Card!" yelled Sakura as she struck the air before her with the Sealing Staff. The entity transformed into a Card with a beautiful woman clad in elegant vines, with the nameplate, 'The Earth.'

A bright light shone from within the bushes nearby, and when it faded, out came a winged lion with a mane of shimmering gold. As he strutted his way toward Sakura, he shot her a triumphant smile.

"Kerberus is back!" bellowed the beast, with a deep voice still bearing that same Kansai accent.

"Kero! This is your true form?" exclaimed Sakura.

"Yep! Supreme, unadulterated coolness am I!"

Sakura threw her arms around the lion and laughed ecstatically, "That means I've caught all the Cards!"

"We still got one more," said Kero, glancing toward the yellow orb still floating about Alice's prone form. They nodded resolutely and marched toward the Witch. As she strutted toward her enemy, Sakura struck the Earth Card, and began to glow with that same brown light. An intense feeling of strength and capability filled her.

The Witch crawled away frantically. She managed to find her serpent staff and blasted Sakura with electricity. The bolts struck her, slid over her body, and crackled into the ground through her feet.

"Don't you know? Electricity always leads to Earth," said Sakura.

Alice blasted her again, and nothing happened. Sakura thrust the Sealing Staff in her face and snapped, "Release the final Card, or I'll take it from you."

Alice sat there dumbstruck, desperately looking for another way to beat the Clow Master. As no more ideas came to mind, she clenched her jaw tighter and tighter. Thick, oozy tears dribbled down her cheeks.

"But, I'm thupothed to win! Mathter thaid I'd win!" she wailed.

"You can't win," said Sakura. "You're just a bully and a meanie. Those never win."

Alice sobbed harder as she held out her hands, and the yellow orb wafted into the air between them. Sakura raised the Sealing Staff and, with a grin, proclaimed, "Return to thine intended form, Clow Card!"

The orb shattered in a crackle of static electricity, before flowing into its inert form. As Sakura took the Card, bearing the image of a fox and the nameplate 'The Thunder,' a feeling of true joy filled her.

"With this, I'm the Master of the Clow," she said.

13 | The Serpent Staff

The area around Tsukimine Shrine was completely cordoned off, and yet that couldn't stop the barrage of people come to see if the rumours were true. Those rumours – that the Cardcaptor was more than a mere fantasy character – spread through the Internet like wildfire the moment the bushes around the shrine caught ablaze. Some described a crazy goth girl throwing Molotov Cocktails around the place; others claimed that there was an electrical fire.

The authorities couldn't even get a straight answer from Sakura, who just wore a smile despite the insanity going on around her. When the police questioned her, she simply said, "Oh, it was very scary when the lights went out and the fire started. But my big, strong, wonderful brother got me out alright."

Yukito had to raise an eyebrow at that, since he often heard Sakura refer to Touya as a brute and a meanie, but never wonderful. Lee scratched his slung arm and coughed in a very blatant manner. A nervous Tomoyo took note, and placed a hand on Sakura's shoulder. "Yes, isn't Touya being nice, compared to the *brute* he usually is?"

Sakura beamed and said, "Oh, but tonight he was simply wonderful, Miss Daidouji!"

Behind her, Lee buried his face in his palm.

The police officer jotted his notes down, trying hard

not to blush at the online celebrity in his presence. It looked like it was almost finished, and he asked, "Just so were clear, you *weren't* trying to capture a Clow Card." Sakura's eyes widened with concern. The officer quickly added, "I mean, for one of your videos? This wasn't a setup to get footage for your videos?"

"Oh, of course not," exclaimed Tomoyo, her hand tightly gripping Sakura's. "We wouldn't dare put people in danger for the sake of a video. Would we, *Sa-ku-ra?*"

"Absolutely not, Miss Daidouji," Sakura chirped.

Lee could have smacked the girl over the head.

Luckily, the officer was convinced and let them go. They darted through the flurry of police, fire fighters, and medics, and kept moving until they were well beyond the ruckus. Yukito stretched and yawned, "Well, wasn't *that* a crazy night. Fancy some crazy girl throwing bombs around. I wonder if I hit my head somewhere. Kept seeing glowing lights and flashes the whole time."

"You'll be fine, Yuki," said Touya. He checked his watch, "It's pretty late. I think we should all head home." He eyed Lee. "Oi, your arm okay?"

"I'll head over to the hospital to get it looked at," said Lee nonchalantly.

Tomoyo piped up, "I'll go with him. Just to make sure he's okay."

Now Touya had an excuse to glare at Sakura, and he said, "Ain't you gonna go too? Make sure your new *friend* is alright?"

Sakura stammered as her eyes darted between Lee and Touya. Tomoyo quickly said, "Oh, it'll be alright. Sakura's had a big night after all. Plus, that hiking trip was really tiring for you. Wasn't it, *Sakura?*"

"Oh yeah," blurted Sakura, feigning a yawn. "I really should get to bed, shouldn't I?"

Lee and Tomoyo took their leave, very glad to be going. Sakura, Touya, and Yukito went the other way toward the nearest bus stop. On the ride home, Yukito was by far the most talkative, and blabbered on about all the wonderful food he hadn't been able to eat at the festival. Touya did his best to stay engaged with his friend, but his attention was pulled elsewhere. He was glad when Yukito went home, and he was alone with his sister.

Sakura faked another yawn and she murmured, "I can't wait to get to bed."

Touya decided he was far enough away from Yukito's house, and he stopped to look fixedly at his sister.

"I really shouldn't be letting strangers into my sister's room, should I?" he said. Sakura glanced back at him with a deadpanned expression. She started to visibly tremble, but was frozen in place. Touya's gaze softened, and with a smile he said, "I know you're not Sakura. But don't worry, I won't hurt you."

The girl relaxed a little, but edged away from him.

"You say that, but aren't you mad for what I did to you?" she murmured.

"I figured you weren't doing that on purpose," said Touya. "Plus, I remember seeing you and Sakura hugging. I guess she saved you from that crazy girl from earlier, right?"

The girl nodded, her gaze fixed downward.

"She hopes you won't bug her about it," she murmured. "She really wants to pretend that nobody saw her secret."

Touya threw his arms up, "Hey, I'm not one to out a magician. Would be pretty hypocritical of me, wouldn't it?"

The girl glanced up in awe of him. She said, "You have powers too? Is that why you knew who I was? Even before I met Master?"

"I can also see our Mum," said Touya with a grin. The girl's jaw dropped in shock. Touya quickly pressed his finger to his lips. "I won't tell, if you won't tell. Deal?"

"Deal," said the girl.

"But I want to add another condition," he said as he

crouched to her level. "You and your buddies all need to look after her, that plush toy of hers included. When I can't keep an eye on her, you have to. Got it?"

The girl beamed, "Got it!"

Touya stood and they started walking. When they got within eyesight of their house, Touya crouched again and said, "Hop on, and pretend you're asleep."

The girl did as she was told, and stayed as still as possible. Touya entered the house, and whispered a few words of assurance to a worried Franklin. He then took the girl to her master's bedroom, laid her on the bed, and turned the lights out.

The girl shot up and retook her true form as the blue-adorned Mirror. She grabbed a rolled futon from the closet and stashed it under the blanket. Just as she stepped back to admire her work, she heard a tapping at the window. She opened it to admit the Fly Card in her avian form.

"I'm sorry I took so long," said Mirror. "Is Master still alright?"

"She's waiting for us, so we'd better hurry," said Fly. Mirror returned to her Card form and wafted into Fly's beak. The bird took flight southeast, Touya's watchful eyes following after it.

* * *

Lee had meant to head straight for the rendezvous point at Tokyo Tower, but Tomoyo overruled him.

"We simply *must* have a costume shoot for Sakura's victory!" she exclaimed. She spent far too long making call after call, Lee all the while growing more annoyed. At the very least, however, he had time to repair his broken forearm with magic.

I have never made such an arrogant blunder in my life, he thought as he recalled the ferocity and ease with which Alice had snapped his arm. He then remembered the skill with which Sakura had defeated the Witch and claimed the final Cards. He smiled as he thought, *Perhaps she **can** pass* *the Final Judgement.*

"All done!" exclaimed Tomoyo, pocketing her phone. "Now we can go to the tower."

"What about your costume?" asked Lee as he binned the now-useless sling.

"My Sakura-Mobile will meet us there," said Tomoyo.

I don't want to know, thought Lee with a shake of his head.

The familiar Daidouji limousine met them at the edge of the park, and drove them to the tower. The hour was late, and the wind was picking up, adding to the chill of the night. Lee kept silent through most of the trip, his eyes fixed on the very large full moon looming overhead.

It will be tonight, thought Lee. *Yue will reveal himself.*

The limousine pulled up beside the NOA Building on Azabudai, still a ways from the tower. As they stood in front of the building, Tomoyo pondered, "Where's Sakura?" At that, the shadows about them came to life, and gathered about their feet. Those shadows started to rise, and lift them upward to the top of the building. They stepped off the umbral elevator and saw Sakura, her green glowing eyes crowning an excited smile. She threw her arms around her friend and cried, "I've gathered all the Cards, Tomoyo! I really did it."

"Congratulations, Sakura," replied Tomoyo. She quickly whipped out her camera and started snapping photos. "I can't wait until the Sakura-Mobile gets here. Then we can take some *real* memorial shots!"

"Sakura-Mobile?" the girl murmured nervously.

"I didn't ask," said Lee.

"Lee, thanks so much for your support," said Sakura warmly. "I wouldn't have been able to beat the Witch if you hadn't trained me."

Lee shuffled gauchely and said, "You're welcome. You did well, Cardcaptor." Sakura bowed, and Lee's mind quickly went to another more pressing matter. "Speaking of the Witch, where is she?"

Sakura pointed the Sealing Staff to a pole, around which a forest of blooming vines were tightly wound. As the trio approached, the vines pulled away to reveal Alice's furious glare. A vine still held itself in her mouth to gag her, so she couldn't speak or shout. All she could do was hiss angrily.

"It was hard gettin' her here, though," said a deep voice behind them. Tomoyo turned and shrieked in surprise. Even Lee was taken aback by the winged lion seated behind them.

"Who might you be?" asked Tomoyo shakily.

The lion rolled his eyes in dismay. "It's me! Kerberus!"

Lee and Tomoyo's jaws dropped.

"Kero?" exclaimed Tomoyo.

Kero struck a pose. "The one and only!"

"Because I captured all the Cards, Kero now has his full power back," Sakura explained.

Lee pursed his lips to stifle a smile as he approached the Beast of the Seal. He said, "I've only seen drawings and paintings of you in this form. But the real thing is impressive."

"You betcha, Brat," snorted Kero. "Next time ya wanna go, I'll take you on like *this*."

"No problem, Fluffy," replied Lee.

Sakura quickly put herself between the two before a fight could start. "So what are we going to do about Alice? To be honest, even with the resonance, Wood and Flower are getting a little tired."

Lee regarded the restrained Witch and the serpent staff leaning against the railing nearby. He picked it up and studied it a moment.

"There are those who would handle something like her," he began. "We really should deliver her to them. But …"

The serpent staff glimmered in his hands. A sinister magical aura emanated from it, sticking to his fingers like molasses. Even a slightest glimpse into its true nature made Lee gag.

"This staff is definitely a facsimile, and would never usurp the Shadow Key," he said. "But it's the best counterfeit I have ever seen. Alice Axolotl is low level Witch, hardly enough to pull off a decent fortune telling." That comment made Alice growl. "When I first knew her, she was scamming seniors with a healing powder that was little more than sand bewitched to glow depending on the holder's sleep debt. Then she was peddling tin-plated plastic as *authentic* Kakugane. Now, she's got a weapon formed from magic so far beyond her. It's like a street busker aping the Ninth Symphony."

"You think somebody else made the staff and gave it to her?" asked Tomoyo.

"She did say her master told her she'd win," said Sakura.

"We need to know who this master is," Lee concluded.

There was a sudden crack, and a searing pain ripped through Sakura's body. She doubled over with a shriek, as the vines flew off Alice. Her body permeated with black discharges, and she grinned evilly. She held up her hand and blasted Tomoyo, knocking her out.

"Now I *know* that's not your magic, Axolotl," snapped Lee. He raised his hands, ready to clap them together. Before they met, Alice suddenly appeared between them, her palm pressed against his chest. A black discharge burst from her hands and knocked him back. He quickly grabbed the ledge of the roof to catch himself.

Alice turned on Sakura, still reeling from Wood's pain. She reached for a Card, but Alice was too fast and delivered a swift uppercut. For Lee, everything slowed down. He saw the path Sakura's limp body followed, and knew it would carry her over the edge of the building.

She's unconscious. I have to save her. I can save her. But why aren't I moving? Move, damn you! Move! If you don't move, she'll die. She's going to die. She's going to ...

She vanished over the edge.

Mortified, Lee screamed, "Sakura![20]"

His anguished cry echoed over the buildings, slowing dying down until there was silence. Alice's cackle permeated that silence, and filled Lee with unyielding rage. That rage mixed with his grief, and immobilised him. That was, until another sound overshadowed the Witch's victory gloat: wing beats.

Up from the edge flew Kero, his wings flapping as they carried him, and Sakura in his arms, above the roof of the building. The pair gazed down at the Witch, who despite her empowering black lightning felt very small. She desperately raised her hand to blast them, but Kero beat her to the punch, and what a punch it was. His fireball smacked her with the full force of his rage, and the Witch flew screaming across the roof. She hit the ground and skidded across the concrete. Still on fire, she scrambled to her feet and snuffed her flaming clothes with a flick of her hand.

Kero set Sakura down on the roof, and the pair strutted toward her again. The Witch glared at them, her raw searing flesh contorted into a horrible countenance. She shot a black lightning bolt, which Sakura swatted aside with her staff. Alice backed away, throwing more bolts that did not make their targets, until she found her back pressed against the ledge of the building. Sakura stopped right in front of the Witch.

"Surrender," she said curtly.

Like a wounded animal cornered, the Witch grit her teeth furiously and bellowed, "Never!" She then swivelled and threw herself off the roof.

Sakura and Kero scrambled to the side of the building, but saw no falling body, no corpse on the sidewalk, no one at all. Sakura reached out with her mind to find the Witch's magical signature, but felt only the coldness of the night.

"Where did she go?" she cried.

20　　In Japan, a man calling a woman by her first name is an assertion of familiarity and intimacy. Lee committed a social faux pas here.

"Dunno! Can't sense her," said Kero irately.

"Can Witches teleport or something?" asked Sakura.

"No, they can't," said Lee. Sakura turned to see him hovering over Tomoyo's body, a healing charm in his hand. Her mind quickly filled with concern for her friend, and she went to nurse Tomoyo while Lee healed her.

"She'll be alright?" asked Sakura. Lee nodded with a warm reassuring smile, but that did little to assuage Sakura's conscience. "I should have protected her," she said. "But when Alice broke through Wood's bindings, I felt that same pain as before. Because I wasn't skilled …"

"Hey, Cardcaptor," said Lee, his hand on her shoulder. "It takes a lot more practice and control to filter the resonance link you share with these Cards. For a while, their pain is going to be yours, and yours theirs."

Kero chimed in, "He's right, ya know. It ain't shameful that you still got trouble. You ain't a superhuman."

"But I couldn't even stop Alice," cried Sakura. "She had that teleportation spell and escaped. Now we won't know who her master is."

Lee laughed, "Witches can't teleport. She probably turned into a salamander and then activated a soul protection spell."

"So they can shapeshift?" asked Sakura. She pondered a moment. "Can I do that?"

"That'd be really cool," said Tomoyo. Sakura looked down and grinned at her friend.

"Tomoyo, how do you feel?" she asked.

"A lot better, thank you," replied the dark haired girl. She glanced at Lee, "Thanks for healing me." Lee bowed with a smile. Tomoyo quickly shot up and gripped her friend's hands. "If Sakura learned how to shapeshift, that'd be the most coolest thing in the world! Lee, you must teach her!"

"I don't think so," said Lee. "Shapeshifting is only something certain beings can do. Despite Sakura's use of magic, she's human. Plus, her magic is of a completely different kind to Alice or mine. Because of that, she's able to wield the Clow Cards."

Far from being disappointed, Tomoyo grew even more excited. "See, Sakura? See how special you are? You're in a completely different league from that Witch."

Lee walked over to where the serpent staff lay on the ground, and studied it a moment. He said, "We've got this staff. My mother and father may be able to find the signature of who made it."

Sakura smiled slightly, and gazed down to her hands still clutched tightly in Tomoyo's. She took stock of the whole night, and with a sigh she said, "Well, I guess its over for now. I've gathered all the Cards, so now I'm the Clow Master."

"This calls for a celebration!" exclaimed Tomoyo. No sooner had she said that did her phone beep. She checked the message, and flew into an even greater paroxysm of joy. She raced to the edge of the roof and saw a yellow van parked by the curb. "The Sakura-Mobile is here!" she cried.

Lee and Tomoyo rode on Kero's back as he and Sakura floated down from the building and landed in an adjacent alley. When they reached the van, Tomoyo sent the chauffeur home in a taxi. She then opened the back door to reveal Tomoyo's entire collection of costumes. Sakura's face went blood red as her friend exclaimed, "You must have an appropriate costume to commemorate this victory!"

Lee and Kero sat outside the van, and tried very hard to ignore the sounds of Tomoyo forcefully changing Sakura into one of the many costumes therein. They rolled their eyes every time Tomoyo screeched, "Doesn't this look darling!" and blushed when they heard Sakura cry, "I can get undressed myself, Tomoyo!"

Fortunately, there was an elephant in the room with which they could distract themselves.

"Yue will come tonight," said Lee.

"Yeah," replied Kero with a sombre look in his golden eyes. "I'm sure that Sakura'll convince him."

The van door opened, and Sakura emerged in a light pink pair of shorts, with a darker pink overcoat, the tails of which reached her ankles. The back of the jacket bore a winged insignia that matched the one Tomoyo used on their YouTube channel.

"Now ain't that a good one!" exclaimed Kero when he saw it. "You've outdone yourself, Tomoyo!"

Lee, by contrast, was speechless. Sakura just stood there, clutching the Sealing Staff, and started to grow nervous under the stare Lee didn't realise he was giving her. That was, until Tomoyo waved her hands in front of his face and said, "You might want to close your mouth before you start drooling, Mister Lee."

Lee quickly straightened himself out and stammered, "Sorry for that! I just … Umm … It looks really good on you."

"Thank you, Lee," said a beaming Sakura.

Tomoyo procured her camera and bellowed, "Now, let us take some commemorative photos!"

Over the next half hour, the camera clicked Sakura in dozens of poses, including ones in which she had the Cards whiz about her, a few with Kero, and even one with Lee. However, in that photo, they stood beside one another, as if they were shy boyfriend and girlfriend on a date. Of course, *that* was purely by Tomoyo's order.

"Ah! This is simply the best," exclaimed the enamoured paparazza.

While Tomoyo had her fun, Sakura just enjoyed the feeling of triumph. She finally had the Cards in her hands. She could feel the soul of each, and they responded to hers. They all felt so happy, and that made her happy. Though, she couldn't shake a tiny twinge of concern, which she traced back to Light and Dark. Then she remembered her earlier confrontation with Kero. She eyed the Beast of the Seal, whose smile belied only worry and a hint of sadness.

Lee had a very similar look, and it told Sakura that he knew too.

"Lee, who's Yue?" she asked.

Lee regarded her with shock. Kero, overhearing the question, hung his head and let his despair show. Even Tomoyo, having seen the sudden change in their expressions, stopped taking pictures. Sakura kept her eyes fixed on Lee, and tried to extend her resonating link out to him as if to read his mind. But she didn't need that to convince him. He already knew he had to tell her.

"Yue is the other of the Guardians of the Clow … The other Beast of the Seal," he said. "And, by the will of Clow, he will make the Final Judgement."

Sakura's heart started to race and she backed away from Lee.

"What does that mean?" asked Tomoyo.

"When the candidate for Master of the Clow, chosen by Kerberus, gathers all the Cards, Yue will appear, and decide if that candidate is worthy," said Lee. "If she is worthy, Yue will anoint her the Master of the Clow. If not …"

"I'll lose the Cards!" exclaimed Sakura. "Kero and the Cards will disappear, won't they?"

"Worse," intoned Kero. "Way, way worse."

Sakura threw her arms around Kero fretfully. "No! I don't want that! You're all my friends! Tell Yue to go away!"

"Can't," said Kero. "This is Clow's will, and I gotta follow it."

"Then train me to pass this Final Judgement," said Sakura flatly. She glanced at Lee, "You can train me just like before."

"No," said Lee, his eyes fixed directly in front of him.

Sakura grit her teeth angrily. "Why not? You said you wanted me to be Master of the Clow. Help me pass!"

"Can't," replied Lee.

"Please!" screamed Sakura.

"Not enough time," intoned Lee. He nodded toward a person across the street and murmured, "He is already here."

Sakura turned, and her jaw dropped in horror. There stood the boy of her dreams, his hands in his jeans pockets, and a blank expression on his face.

Sakura mumbled, "Yukito?"

14 | The Final Judgement

Silvery filaments flowed around Yukito, growing and contorting together until they enveloped him in white light. When the glare cleared, there stood another figure, bedizened with an ornate changsham robe. A sapphire encrusted headdress held back his long silver hair, and a large pendant of nephrite jade hung from his neck. He spread his wings as if to stretch them out after a long slumber. With a sigh, he opened his eyes, and set his reptilian orbs upon Sakura.

Sakura gazed with stinging eyes. Terrified, she murmured, "Who is that?"

"He's Yue," said Kero with a sneer.

Yue's bare feet left the ground and his wings carried him across the street to the group. Tomoyo withdrew from the being as he landed before them, and stared down his nose at Sakura.

Lee backed away, his eyes trained on Yue as he prised Sakura's terrified hands away from his arm. The girl could only silently protest as she was left to stand under Yue's piercing gaze. She couldn't hold eye contact with him long before she started to sob.

One side of Yue's lips upturned as his gaze shifted to the winged lion.

"It has been too long, Kerberus," he said. The sound

of his voice, so much like Yukito's and yet strident as sand paper, sent chills down Sakura's spine. He hardly took note of Sakura backing away, and the camera-wielding girl who put herself between him and her.

"Age hasn't liven'd you up, has it, Yue?" replied Kero. "I'd thought you'd've gotten a little cooler in ya golden years, considerin' you'd been couped up in that Yukito kid's skin."

"What do you mean, Kero?" exclaimed Sakura. "What happened to Yukito?"

Yue looked over his shoulder and said, "Nothing. I am Yukito, and Yukito is I. Through his eyes, I have acquainted myself with the candidate chosen by my counterpart." He drew near to her, Tomoyo and Lee pushed aside by an unseen force in his wake. He studied her trembling form, cradling her chin in his hand. His skin was smooth, without blemish, more so than Yukito. It glimmered in the pale moonlight.

The realisation dawned on Sakura.

"The golden lion on the front of the Book of Clow," she exclaimed. "That was Kero. Then, you're the silver moon on the back. I met you a month after I opened the book and became the Cardcaptor."

"I awoke at that moment, and went to where I could gather my strength and don a disguise," said Yue. "Then I manoeuvred myself to be as close to you as possible."

Sakura's heart froze in her chest. Her skin tingled with fear. Her every mental image of Yukito's captivating smile revealed a hidden thicket of nettles, tearing at her mind. Grieved tears threatened to burst from her eyes.

"Yukito wasn't real?" she mumbled. "My number one wasn't real."

"He was a disguise, but a separate soul I fashioned to conceal my own," said Yue with an absolute deadpanned tone. "Though, I must say, it was not as easy as I initially expected. Yukito is a difficult steed to wrangle."

Sakura's mouth flew open in shock.

"Does that mean, you're not really him?" she asked.

"In a sense, that is true," said Yue. When Sakura sighed with relief, his brow furrowed and he glared at Kero. "Kerberus, your candidate is not adequate. She lacks understanding of magic, has limited combat capability, and could not obtain all the Cards on her own. Not only did she require assistance from a descendant of Clow, but from a mere photographer lacking any magical prowess of her own." Yue huffed at the presence of Lee and Tomoyo – especially Lee. "A magician of *his* level, a relative of Clow Reed? The notion sickens me," he spat.

"Yue, you're an ass," said Kero.

"And you're a fool if you think this *weakling* is a fitting master," snapped Yue, his voice not raising above a whisper. "I, Yue, have concluded the Final Judgement. Sakura Kinomoto will *not* be our new master."

Tomoyo finally spoke up, her nerves having reached breaking point. "How can you say that!?" she snapped. "How dare you pass judgement on a girl you don't even know!?"

At first, Yue acted as if no one had said a thing. Then his eyeballs rotated in their sockets to shot beams at her.

"I *do* know her," he said. "Through Yukito, I have seen her incompetence, her idiocy, and her attention-seeking behaviour. Treating the Clow Cards like toys and garnering notoriety with them." His voice grew faster, more fervent, and reached the volume of a low growl. "It is an insult to my true master!" He swivelled, his hand outstretched to Sakura, "Hand over the Clow Cards."

"No!" snapped Sakura, clutching the deck of Cards in her pocket.

Lee suddenly flicked Yue's outstretched palm aside.

"*Huǒ shén zhāolái!*[21]" he roared, and a red flash burst from his hand. Yue flew into the air, over Kero's head, and tumbled along the street. A twinge of elation filled Lee,

---

[21] Mandarin: "Fire God, Come Forth!"

and he grinned. That grin vanished when the being stood, unharmed, with Lee's ball of fire floating harmlessly before him. With a clench of his fist, he snuffed it.

"Fool," mumbled Yue. His eyes darted to the side, and an invisible hand gripped the scruff of Lee's shirt. With a shocked grunt, he flew headfirst into the costume van and crumpled to the ground.

"Lee!" cried Sakura, lunging for him.

Tomoyo caught her and pushed her back. "Sakura, run for it!"

"Useless," mumbled Yue. That same force gripped Tomoyo and threw her into the wall.

Sakura's legs turned to jelly as the lunar being sauntered toward her, his hand once again outstretched.

I have to run, she thought panicked. *But I can't move. I can't fight Yukito! I don't want to fight anyone!*

"If my mere presence terrifies you so, it is merely more evidence that you are unfit," said Yue.

"Hang on, one darned minute, Yue!" snapped Kero. The lion spread his wings and he rose to his full height. Through the haze of her fear, Sakura saw Kero stare down Yue. The Beast of the Seal gritted his teeth and roared, "By the will of Clow!"

For the first time, Yue showed a glimmer of unease.

"You and me used to say that, eh?" said Kero. "Whenever there was somethin' Clow wanted us to do, but we had no clue why, we'd say, 'By the will of Clow!'" Kero nodded toward Sakura. "I am the Selector, and *I* chose Sakura, 'cause I like her. *You* are the Judge! And you promised Clow you'd be fair. So, by the will of Clow, be fair, dammit!"

Yue's lips pursed tighter and tighter with every word Kero belched, and his brow knitted tighter with increasing fury. Finally, he relaxed and said, "Very well, Kerberus. If it will shut you up, I will follow the will of our *true* master." He glanced at Sakura and his eyes glowed blue.

Sakura blacked out. In the next instant, she was

standing on a rooftop right in front of Tokyo Tower. The chilly midnight wind blew about her, wafting her cape around as if she were a superhero ready for the decisive battle. But she hardly felt as such. Yue stood amid the scaffolding above the tower's observation deck, his wings spread like a predator ready to strike. Despite being far away, she could hear his voice in her mind, and so could the Clow Cards.

"Cards created by Clow," Yue proclaimed. At his utterance, the Cards flew from Sakura's pocket and girdled her. "Here stands before you one wishing to be our master. She has been chosen by Kerberus the Selector. By the will of Clow, I, Yue the Judge, will now carry out the Final Judgement."

The Cards flashed spectacularly, before arranging themselves into a neat deck in Sakura's hand. She gauchely gazed up at Yue, shivering at the coldness of the wind and that of his radiating blue stare.

"What do I do?" she asked.

"With the Cards in your hand, defeat me," he ordered.

"What do you mean, *defeat you?*" she exclaimed. "You mean, fight? I can't!"

"Then you will not be my master," retorted Yue.

"I don't want to become a master by hurting someone," exclaimed Sakura. "I didn't even want to hurt Alice Axolotl. How can I hurt you, Yue? How can I hurt Yukito?"

Yue raised his hand, his eyes flashed blue, and he murmured, "Bring her to me, Fly."

Fly sped from her place in the deck and transformed into wings upon Sakura's back. The girl shrieked as the wings dragged her through he air. She reached out through the resonance to Fly, but her mind found only an ethereal brick wall. Fly brought her to the top of the observation deck and callously dropped her to the metal surface, before returning to her inert form in the deck. Sakura pulled her bewildered self to her feet and glanced over at

Yue.

"You will fight, or you will fail the Final Judgement," said Yue.

"Then what? You'll try to take the Cards away?" exclaimed Sakura.

"No, they will leave of their own accord," said Yue. "By the will of Clow, if the candidate cannot defeat me, the Cards must abandon that candidate."

"No," shrieked Sakura.

"Then defeat me," snapped Yue. He held his hands up in front of the nephrite pendant around his neck, and a bright beam of energy shot from within it. Sakura struck the Shield Card just in time, but the beam hit harder than anything she'd felt before. She almost fell off the tower. She quickly activated the Jump Card and launched into the scaffolding of the tower.

Hanging from a horizontal beam, she cried, "I won't let you take the Cards away from me. They're my friends."

"Then have them fight with you!" snapped Yue.

"No! I won't hurt Yukito," replied Sakura. "You're in there somewhere, I know it. Wake up, Yukito! Take your body back from him!"

"Fool!" growled Yue. With a wave of his hands, a bow formed of pure energy appeared before him. He pulled back on the bow and loosed a barrage of ethereal blasts at Sakura. Panicked, Sakura darted out of the way, but couldn't avoid an energy arrow striking her calf. She wailed in pain as her resonance link to Jump failed and she crashed hard against the metal floor. Yue launched another attack, and Sakura cast Fly.

Yue's eyes narrowed furiously as the girl fled. "You will not convince me by fleeing!" His wings spread and he flew after her.

Kero landed on the building adjacent to the tower, shouldering Tomoyo and Lee. The three gazed up at the magical battle going on inside the tower. Tomoyo was so horrified she couldn't bring herself to record the fight.

"Yue is a truly hateful person," she stammered, wincing with every blow Yue dealt her friend. Tears trickled down her cheeks.

"He's mean-spirited, for sure," said Kero. "And he's stubborn too. But there's another side to him, and I know Sakura can reach it."

"And if she can't!" growled Lee, a cocktail of fear and fury smeared across his face.

"She will," replied Kero in a faint whisper. In his mind, he roared, *Come on, girl! Show him!*

Sakura darted in and out of the tower's structure, her senses fixed on Yue's signature, closing in on her fast. She cast out Mirror, who took on her guise and bounded through the framework to charge Yue, Sword in her hand. Yue nonchalantly dodged her blow and gripped her neck.

"I share the same resonance link with the Cards as you," said his voice in Sakura's panicked mind. "Thus, I know when Mirror is near." With a growl, Yue slammed Mirror into a vertical beam. A blunt jolt of pain electrified through the link and struck Sakura's back. Her wings disappeared, and her momentum carried her into another beam, which she struck hard. Her shoulder seared from the impact, and her mind spun so much she could hardly get a grip on which way was up.

Yue didn't let up. He sped through the air toward Sakura and kicked her in the stomach. She flew through the framework and out the side of the tower. Yue moved with lightning speed, and caught her mid-air. He then threw her by her hair back into the tower, where she struck another vertical beam. He landed beside her flailing form, gripped her by the scruff of her neck and threw her into another beam.

Sakura crumpled unceremoniously onto a maintenance walkway. Almost every part of her body ached, and those that didn't were numb. She gripped the Sealing Staff, and thought frantically.

I have to beat Yue, or he'll kill me and take the Cards. But how can I do it? He's too strong.

She looked at her surroundings, and remembered her first video shooting. Then she remembered the events that video had been based on. She breathed deeply and steeled herself. Then she pushed past the pain in her extremities and drew two Cards.

"Become binding chains! Windy! Wood!" she cried as she struck the two Cards. Windy and Wood burst from the wand, but Sakura could not feel their resonance link. Suddenly, a flurry of vines and wind gusts enveloped her, wound themselves around her arms and legs, and squeezed her. They lifted her into the air and presented her to Yue.

The other Beast of the Seal sneered at her. "Like I said, I have the same resonance link as you do. No matter what Card you use, you will never overpower me. No one but Clow can be my master."

Down below, Kero, Tomoyo, and Lee could hear Yue's sinister voice.

"The candidate has failed the Final Judgement," he almost gloated. "Kerberus the Selector has chosen poorly, and thus, the Clow Cards will be returned to their slumber."

"No!" cried Sakura. "Don't leave me!"

"And when they do," Yue continued, smirking as if he were relishing the thought. "When they do, the world as you know it will end."

Sakura's heart stopped. Horror filled her as she desperately sought breath. When she couldn't, Tomoyo's voice filled her mind and asked, "What does that mean?"

"The resonance link you share with the Cards carries more than instructions and magical nourishment," said Yue. "It also carries your essence. By achieving resonance with the Cards, they have imprinted upon you, and have come to love you. If you cannot be their master, then they must sever that resonance. To do so will require a fee of equal value."

"Equal value?" stammered Sakura.

"All the memories of most precious loved ones," said Kero. "And it ain't just Sakura's either."

"All of the people who came in contact with the Clow Cards will forget about everyone precious to them," droned Lee.

Tomoyo gasped in horror, her camera falling to the ground and shattering.

"Takeshi bought the Sword Card when he thought it was a broach," she whispered tearfully. "Chiharu was controlled by the Sword Card. Naoko and our entire class were attacked by the Illusion Card. Mom and I and all our house staff met the Shield Card. All the people who were attacked when that Witch set the Mirror Card on a rampage. All the people in the aquarium who saw Watery. Every single person who watched our Cardcaptor videos online. Millions of people!"

"Everyone will forget," droned Sakura.

Lee glared up at the tower, and prepared to smack his hands together.

"I won't let this happen!" he shrieked.

A paw gripped the back of his head and pushed him into the ground.

"Ya try that, and it really will be the end!" snapped Kero as he held him down tightly. He gazed up at the tower, tears very near to his eyes.

Come on, girl! Show him!

Sakura thrashed desperately in the hijacked embrace of Windy and Wood. She reached out to the Cards through the resonance link, which she found deafeningly silent. Grief infiltrated her mind like a slow-acting poison, sapping her strength as she wailed, "They can't forget! I won't let them forget!"

The world around her started to dim, the colours about her growing dull. The vines constricted her, and clamped down on her chest until she could no longer breathe. Light started to fade around her, until all that remained was the dwindling luminance of Yue's eyes. The ire in his gaze remained strong in that light, and yet, to Sakura's fading consciousness, it seemed tainted ever so slightly with sorrow.

Yukito? Are you sad? Are you fighting against Yue for me?

An image of her father crept into her mind, gazing at the photo on the dining table. Before it lay a fresh corsage of nadeshiko flowers, which Franklin stroked with a warm smile.

"Good morning, my dear," he said. Within the cheerful harmonics of his voice, Sakura could sense the same sorrow that was in Yue's gaze.

No, Yukito's not sad … Yue is.

"There's someone he misses," said someone. In the void of Sakura's last scraps of awareness, she turned to see the woman in her father's photo.

"Mum?" she murmured.

Nadeshiko grinned, "Hello, Sakura. It's been too long."

Sakura beamed with delight, and threw her arms around her mother. She giggled at how much bigger she remembered her mother, and revelled in the chance to see her again. Then she remembered why she hadn't seen her in so long, and a realisation gripped her.

"Am I dead?" she asked.

Nadeshiko burst into laughter. "You could not be more alive. And I couldn't be more proud of my cherry-blossom."

Sakura looked around the void, reminded of when she confronted the Dark Card, and asked, "Then how are you here?"

"I've always been here, keeping an eye on you," said Nadeshiko. "Though I would have done it anyway, someone asked me to come look after you when you found the Book of Clow."

Sakura's brow furrowed. "Who?"

A field of stars formed in the void. At first, only a few were visible, then more appeared, until the space about their feet was replete with the stars of an entire galaxy.

Amazed, Sakura glanced around at the distant galaxies emerging from the space around her.

Nadeshiko smiled and indicated a figure seated amid the star field. The Chinese man looked up from his book and gazed at them. His simple purple robe glimmered as he bowed to Sakura with a smile.

A serene voice filled her mind, "Thank you for gathering my children, and being such a good friend to them. I know you will take the best of care of them."

*Children? I'm not looking after any children ... unless you mean the Clow Cards. Does that mean you're **him**?*

The man's smile widened as he turned back to his book. Sakura started walking toward him, her mind filled with curiosity. Her mother's hand on her shoulder stopped her.

"You'll get to see him soon enough, Sakura," said Nadeshiko. "Right now, you have a bigger problem."

Sakura frowned, having completely forgotten where she was. Her eyes widened in realisation.

"I failed the Final Judgement," she exclaimed. "Everyone who saw my videos will forget their loved ones!"

"Not yet, you haven't," retorted Nadeshiko. "You can still beat him."

"How? He's too powerful and just overwhelms my resonance with the Cards!"

"Think!" said Nadeshiko. "How did you get here? What did you see in him that brought you here?"

Sakura thought back, and remembered the truly solemn gleam in Yue's eyes.

"He was so sad," she mumbled. "He said no one but Clow could be his master."

"But Clow is here, where I am," said Nadeshiko. "And he won't come back. Yue hasn't accepted that. You'll have to make him."

"How? He's so stubborn and won't listen," exclaimed Sakura.

"Overpower him and make him listen," said Nadeshiko. "Resonate with the Cards, overshadow him with your power, and show him you're worthy."

Uncertainty still held Sakura by the short hairs, and she couldn't think of any way she could win. She gazed up at her mother, not remotely as tall as she remembered. Nadeshiko kissed her forehead and said, "Remember your invincible spell."

Sakura smiled, and her hesitation vanished.

"I'll definitely be alright!" she said resolutely.

The stars about her brightened until their light filled her gaze, before peeling back like a curtain and revealing the world around her. A shockwave burst from her body, throwing off Wood and Windy. She quickly reached through the resonance link, now clearer than glass, and grabbed hold of their souls.

A wave of surprise, even fright, crashed over Yue as the blast threw him back. He smacked his head against the tower's framework, and had to land to recover from the dizziness and ringing in his ears. Dazed, he glanced up to a light more dazzling than the Moon above.

Sakura floated amid the framework, her luminescent green eyes fixed on him as the Cards circled about her. They fell to her feet and made a walkway across which she strutted toward him. He reached out with his mind, but could not breach the barrier she'd erected out of nothing.

"Yue," Sakura proclaimed. "That's enough mischief."

Yue growled and shot into the air. He let loose a barrage of arrows that dinged harmlessly against Shield. He then summoned a sword of pure energy and charged her. With the Sword Card, she parried his every blow. With Earth, she summoned the strength to throw him into a vertical beam and hold him there. Yue freed himself with a blast from his pendant that Sakura had to evade. Luckily, Jump and Fly were at the ready to give her a speed boost, and carried her safely to the maintenance walkway.

Yue landed on the walkway and charged her. He

slashed through her, but she dissolved into a fractal pattern. He swivelled just in time to parry her roundhouse kicks and punches; just managing in time to land his own blow only to realise he was fighting Mirror. A barrage of shadowy spikes lunged at him from the sides, which he defeated with a bright flash of light from his eyes. His every muscle suddenly tensed with a burning jolt of electricity that surged through the metal walkway and into his bare feet. He staggered, growling and grunting at the pain. He managed to push himself up from the walkway floor and saw his enemy, twirling the Sealing Staff as if it was a gymnast's baton. He scrambled to his feet and dashed forward, only to slip on a pile of flower petals and fall face-first onto the floor. In his infuriated daze, he didn't sense the incoming attack until the fireball hit him. The Fiery Card gripped him in his flaming tendrils, lifted him above the floor and threw him over the edge of the walkway, head-first into a floating ball of water. Watery took hold of him and twirled him around, before sending him flying out of the tower's framework.

Overwhelmed and infuriated, Yue spread his wings to stop his ballistic flight and glared back at Sakura in the tower. She spread her wings to match his height.

"You think you can muster a little resolve and that's it?" Yue bellowed. He raised his hands to his pendant once more, but Sakura was faster.

She struck two Cards and cried, "Trap the fiend standing yonder! Windy! Wood!"

The pair of elementals burst from their Cards with gusto, and enveloped a bewildered Yue. He struggled and thrashed as they dragged him toward their beloved master. Sakura struck one more Card, and Yue was thrown into a void. Windy and Wood no longer gripped him, and he was able to move freely. Of course, he couldn't see where he was. He couldn't even see his own body in the darkness.

"The Dark is chief among my subordinates!" he snapped. He reached out with his mind to lock onto the

Card's soul, but once again found only a barrier. He reached out again with more force, hoping to break that wall, but only grew more frustrated. "Why?" he exclaimed. "Why will you not respond? Dark!"

Sakura's voice sounded, "I guess she likes me more. I'm nice."

Yue straightened his posture in an effort to calm himself, but his body would not stop shaking.

"You mean to hold me hostage until I acknowledge you?" he bellowed. "You cannot force such companionship. That is slavery."

"And I wouldn't dream of it, Mister Yue," said Sakura, though she was still invisible. "I don't want to enslave anyone. And, to be honest, I don't really like the idea of being a master, either."

Yue scoffed, "Why then undergo this judgement? Why gather the Cards?"

Sakura giggled, "Because I like them. They're such nice people. And quirky too. I hang out with Tomoyo all the time, and she stalks me with a video camera and posts videos of me without my permission, but I can't be without her. Kero steals my allowance for sweets that he doesn't share with me, but it's just too much fun watching him gorge himself. And when I first met Lee, he beat me up, but he showed me he really is nice … though I think he might be a gambler." A seedling of light appeared to illuminate Sakura's face in the darkness. "Takeshi makes up stories, Chiharu smacks him for it, Naoko is a fantasy nerd, my Big Brother's a meanie, and my Dad will never remarry because he loves my Mum too much."

Sakura drew near to Yue in the darkness, and locked eyes with him. She kept her smile while he returned a stoic glare.

"I love quirky people," she continued. "Even Yukito, the most gorgeous man alive, who could eat ten-times his body weight and still be hungry."

Yue chuckled, surprising himself.

"I don't want to be a master and order you around or anything," said Sakura. "I just want to be your friend. And I think you want that too. Because you miss it." Yue said nothing. "You miss Clow, don't you? You loved him, didn't you? I'm not going to try and replace him. I don't think I could. But I can be a different kind of master for you all. Even you, because though you're violent and stubborn, you're just so much like Yukito, I couldn't help but love you. I want you to be my friend."

Yue's glare did not waver, nor did he move for a while. Then he growled, "Damn you, Clow." To the girl before him, he said, "We're done. Restore the world."

Sakura disabled the Dark and Light, and the world reappeared around them.

A very grumpy Yue spread his wings and proclaimed, "The Final Judgment is complete. I, Yue the Judge, hereby acknowledge Sakura Kinomoto as Master of the Clow."

15 | Master of the Clow

When Sakura came to, she found herself standing on an asphalt walkway. Above her hung reams of *koinobori*[22] suspended on cables that led away from the building behind her. She strained her neck and saw Tokyo Tower reaching into the sky above. She looked down in bewildered thought, recalling her last memory.

I, Yue the Judge, hereby acknowledge Sakura Kinomoto as Master of the Clow.

"Yue accepted me. I beat him, and convinced him," she droned, her mind filled with shock.

She heard footsteps to her left and turned to see Tomoyo and Lee racing toward her. The sight snapped her out of her reverie, and a wide involuntary smile appeared on her face.

"I did it!" she screamed.

Overjoyed, Tomoyo threw her arms around her friend and squeezed her tightly.

"Oh, my dear Sakura! You saved the world!" exclaimed Tomoyo.

Sakura beamed, and gripped her friend's hands tightly. "Did you get it on tape?"

---

22 Carp-shaped flags

Tomoyo gasped in horror. "I should have! But I was so shocked by what Yue threatened, I dropped my camcorder and it broke!"

"Oh no! But we can get another one and record a new video," said Sakura.

Tomoyo's eyebrows shot up the length of her forehead and she said, "You actually want to do more videos?"

"Of course! And I'm sure Yue and Kero would love to help," exclaimed Sakura.

Tomoyo's eyes glimmered with excitement and she cried, "Ah! My dear Sakura is going to be a star!" She proceeded to dance around the place and plot various schemes for the next series of *Cardcaptor Sakura*. Meanwhile, Lee stepped forward.

"Congratulations, Cardcaptor," he said with a bow.

Sakura looked at him, and recalled a moment not too long before. Though a great deal of fear accompanied that memory, something in it made her heart swell warmly. She looked fixedly into his eyes with a grin.

"Before, when Alice threw me off the roof, you called me 'Sakura,'" she said.

Lee stammered, "I'm sorry. That was rude and I shouldn't have."

"Not at all," said Sakura with a giggle. "It felt nice." That made Lee blush slightly, but not enough for Sakura to notice. Then she said, "Hey, can I call you by your first name?" Now *that* made him blush profusely.

"If you want to," he replied in a low whisper.

"Then … hey, I don't even know your first name," said Sakura. "Alice called you Coyote. Is that it?"

Lee chuckled, "No, that's just a code name I'm known by. My real name is Xiaolang."

"Xiaolang," Sakura murmured. Then she beamed, "Nice to meet you, Xiaolang."

Lee's tongue caught in his throat and he could barely grind out a response of, "Nice to meet you too, Sakura."

Suddenly, a flying teddy bear plopped itself onto

Sakura's head and a familiar squeaky voice resounded, "See there, Brat? I told ya Sakura'd pass!" He knocked on Sakura's forehead and said, "Hey, Sakura, did ya know this dumb Brat thought ya wouldn't pass? Pah! No faith in girls, he has. Sexist, I'd say."

Kero started a victory dance on Sakura's head. Lee rolled his eyes, while Sakura was more pensive.

"You knew, didn't you?" she asked. "You both knew what was going to happen, didn't you?"

Kero stopped his dance and fell into a frenzy of stammers, while Lee backed away slightly, his eyes diverted.

"Forgive me," said Lee. "Not to divert blame, but Kerberus begged me not to tell you. I wanted to, because I thought it was important that you were ready. But he insisted."

Sakura looked up, displacing the plush toy from her head, and glared at him. Kero finally gave up, and floated down to look at his new master.

"I'm sorry, Sakura," he said as his head drooped. "I blew off my guardian duty and was asleep. Then ya got the Cards while my guard was down, and before I knew it, ya were in the deep end. I was scared that, if I told ya, you'd back out and the Cards would just ruin the world anyway. And how could I do that to ya? How could I wreck the life of a girl with so much wonderful stuff goin' on around ya? Tomoyo, Fibber-Boy, Fibber-Boy's-girlfriend, Hermione-cosplay-girl, ya bro, Snow Rabbit, ya Dad and even ya Mom. Ya only captured the Cards because ya had fun. If you'd known what'd happen if ya failed, ya'd be always worried, and wouldn't've just lived ya life."

Kero kept his eyes fixed on the ground, certain that Sakura was angry and desperate to not see it in her face. Then he heard her voice, "Kero, look at me." His eyes very reluctantly drifted up to meet hers, which crowned a wide smile. Then she hugged his small form and said, "Thanks so much for having my back."

"I'm so glad you won," said Kero, gripping her tighter. Still holding her friend, Sakura looked to Lee with a warm smile and said, "Thanks for training me, Xiaolang."

Lee just smiled in response.

Kero, on the other hand, burst out of the embrace and bellowed, "Xiaolang? You're on a first name basis with this brat? Since when?"

"Since two minutes ago," replied Sakura. "It's okay."

"It's so totally *not* okay!" snapped Kero. "I'll never allow you to be so close with this brat!"

"Why? Afraid she'll like me more than a fluffy glutton like you?" retorted Lee.

"You wanna go, Brat!" roared Kero, his clenched fists ready for a fight.

The verbal blows went back and forth in front of Sakura, who could only grin nervously. Tomoyo drew up beside her and said, "We thought it'd be over, but it looks like the fun's just getting started."

"Why do you say that?" asked Sakura.

"Tsukishiro most definitely has a love rival," murmured Tomoyo. Her excited, gossip-hungry smile made the blood drain from Sakura's face.

"No, no, no! Xiaolang and I are just friends," exclaimed Sakura. "I still love Yukito."

At that moment, a heavenly voice reached her ears. It said, "Who's talking about me behind my back?"

Sakura swivelled to see Yukito, in his regular jeans and jacket, a knowing smile on his face.

"Yukito! You're back!" she exclaimed. "You're not —"

Yukito pressed his finger to his lips to shush her. Then he crouched to look up at her and said, "I'm sorry for lying to you and keeping this all a secret. There were so many times I wanted to tell you, to warn you. But I couldn't. The Other Guy wouldn't let me, unfortunately." He smiled. "I will say, though, I'm really grateful to him. Otherwise, I wouldn't have met you or Touya. And I promise you, even though Yue doesn't look it, he is glad to have you as his master. So am I."

Sakura beamed, her heart racing at the praise her Number One dished out. Before she could say anything further, Yukito quickly added, "Also, I get to be in the Cardcaptor videos!"

"Oh, the Cardcaptor videos are going to be amazing!" exclaimed Tomoyo. "We can do movies and side plots, and you're all going to be stars!"

"It's gonna be legendary," roared Kero.

"This is ridiculous," murmured Lee, an excited grin on his face.

Tomoyo thrust her finger into the air and proclaimed, "I must take a group shot to commemorate Sakura becoming Master of the Clow!" She reached into her backpack and procured a tripod for her DLSR. While she set it up under Kero's curious gaze, Yukito took Sakura aside.

"I'd like to ask a favour," he said. "Could you not tell Touya about this? It's really important."

"Of course not," replied Sakura. "If he found out about this, I'd never hear the end of it. Plus my Dad would find out and they'd never let me leave the house."

Yukito grinned, "I'm so glad I met you and him."

"Likewise," replied Sakura.

Tomoyo announced she was ready. Sakura dragged Lee and Yukito into the frame. Tomoyo pressed the button, and she and Kero raced toward the group.

"Everyone smile!" said Sakura.

From the shadows near the tower, Touya watched his sister and her friends snap pictures and reminisce. A smile rode on his face, which Nadeshiko picked up on and said, "You knew that he wasn't human, didn't you?"

"Yep," said Touya, his grin widening.

"And yet you're still friends with him," said Nadeshiko. Touya said nothing in reply, the unspoken meaning of his silence reaching her. She placed her hand on his shoulder and said, "I think he's a wonderful boy."

Touya turned to her and said, "Thanks, Mum. And thanks for helping Sakura out." Nadeshiko smiled. With a dash of disappointment to his voice, Touya said, "So, I suppose you'll be going back to wherever you call home?"

Nadeshiko pursed her lips thoughtfully. "Not yet."

* * *

Alice fell to her feet, sobbing and wailing, as the being with yellow reptilian eyes glared at her from the shadows.

"Pweathe forgive my faiwure, mathter!" she cried. "I did evewything I could, *dopyuu!*"

"You couldn't defeat that little girl, even with the strongest of the Cards," snapped the figure.

Alice suddenly started to wail and writhe in pain, black sparks rippling along her body.

"Pweathe, thtop! Mathter!" she moaned.

"What infuriates me is that you left the staff I gave you!" spat the being. "Coyote will no doubt take that staff back to his family, and they will find me. *My* cover is potentially blown because of your incompetence."

"But I therved you tho wew, mathter!" exclaimed Alice. "I wiw do aw I can to make it up to you. Jutht, pweathe don't kiw me! Pweathe!"

The being stopped whatever it was doing to her, and she fell limp on the concrete. It pondered a moment as Alice pulled herself to her feet, hunched and nursing her sore limbs.

"Very well," said the being. "You *did* capture seven of the Cards, and they were some of the most powerful. And you showed unflinching loyalty in your conduct with me. So, as a courtesy, I won't kill you."

Relief flooded Alice's heart and she prostrated before the being, "Oh, thank you, mathter! You awe twuwy a gweat perthon."

"Flattery won't get you far," said the being. "Our working relationship is terminated."

"Ath you wish, mathter," said Alice as she turned to

leave. Another figure, in a black dress, blocked the alleyway exit. The figure's faint purple hair dully refracted the moonlight. Confused, Alice glanced back at the shadow, who said, "Like I said, *I* won't kill you."

The figure grinned psychotically as he slashed his hand on a damaged pipe, and a black substance gushed from the wound. Alice watched, horrified at her impending doom, as the black blood formed a broadsword in the figure's hand.

The sword gurgled ravenously.

Epilogue

Autumn had just started to set in, and the British countryside, a deep green in summer, was turning red. Dried leaves cluttered the windshield of the black, unmarked car as it pulled up to the gates of a mansion. The rustic retreat seemed modest, considering the wealth and influence of the man who lived there. Of course, the car's occupant knew that modesty meant inconspicuousness, which, in their mutual lines of work, was godliness.

The driver announced their presence at the intercom, and the gates admitted them. The passenger emerged from the vehicle, and brushed a fallen leaf from the 'A' embroidered on his lapel. A maid came to greet him, and led him into the mansion. He followed her through the house that smelled of scented candles and a hint of smoke, and arrived at a small study.

At the desk sat a young boy, barely older than sixteen, with a twinge of red to his hair, betraying his Scottish descent. The man stood before the boy, and felt a tad perplexed that he, a military man with decades of experience, was deferential to a child of such scant years.

His body, maybe, but not his mind, he reminded himself.

"Announcing, Master, General Piers Rodrigo of the Alchemic Regiment," said the maid. She turned to him and said, "General, allow me to present Eriol Lamperouge."

The General bowed, but the boy didn't respond. He finished his writing, read his work over, then packaged it in an envelope, sealed it with wax, and passed it to his maid.

"Please have this delivered, Ruby," he said. "That will be all."

"At once, Master," said Ruby and she quickly left, shutting the doors behind her.

Eriol looked at the General with deep, piercing eyes.

"How long has it been, General?" he murmured.

"We've never met," replied Rodrigo.

"Wasn't asking that," replied Eriol. "We've not met. But *I've* met your organisation. I believe it was 1760? One of your less savoury predecessors approached me about assistance in your war with the homunculi. I told him, in not so blunt terms, to go to Hell."

"I'm not here about Restigouche," said Rodrigo. "I'm here to confirm something."

Eriol irately fidgeted in his seat and snapped, "Go to Hell. You're not getting them."

"I'm not asking for them, Lord Lamperouge," Rodrigo insisted. "I merely want to confirm that they have fallen under a new master."

"They have, and she's not joining you," retorted Eriol. "She's not the kind of person who belongs in a war with monsters or reaping souls."

Rodrigo opened his mouth to retort, but swallowed his words and thought a moment.

"Have you already been approached?" he asked.

"The Reaper's little boy visited yesterday," said Eriol. "I spoke to him outside the boundaries of the estate. I was afraid he'd start making my house symmetrical and even add another room onto it to ensure there was a multiple of eight. But I told him the same for both: go to Hell."

Rodrigo gritted his teeth, almost offended that someone as great as Clow Reed could reincarnate himself as such an obnoxious Scot. It took all his will power to not stroke the Kakugane in his pocket. With a deep breath, he collected his thoughts and said, "Very well. I merely wished to confirm the Clow Cards have a new master, and that the threat they posed was neutralised. I will take my leave."

He turned to go, but was barely within reach of the door before it locked with a spark. Eriol rose from his chair and walked toward the General, a twinge of curiosity in his eyes.

"Why not then get one of your lackeys to do it?" he asked. "Why come all the way into the middle of Glastonbury to ask something you could have done over the phone?"

Got him, thought the General.

"We may need her help," said Rodrigo. "We've located Victor."

Eriol's eyes darkened, and any rivalry he felt for the man went far to the back of his mind.

"Where?" he asked.

"Australia, in a town called Wollongong," said Rodrigo.

"Has he reached his full strength?"

"It seems he hasn't, but Doctor Butterfly is a talented alchemist, and he will figure it out," said Rodrigo. "Captain Bravo, the Spartan Valkyrie, and the Starlight Lancer are stationed there, and are investigating. But if things go sour, we may need help." Eriol thought for a moment, but said nothing. The General went on, "Listen, you don't like our organisation, or the Reaper's, and I understand why. We're not trying to steal the Clow Cards or undermine you. We just need –"

"It's alright, I understand," Eriol interjected.

"Can we count on the Cardcaptor's help?" asked Rodrigo.

Eriol sighed, well aware of the stakes. Such a force as Victor was nothing to trifle with, or to disregard for the sake of petty squabbles from the past. That much, Eriol knew, and was grateful that his predecessor had, at the very least, given him that logical part of his personality. And yet, he couldn't shake the fear of what would come from joining forces with these people, or what might happen to Sakura.

This is too important to ignore, he concluded. *But it's too big for her to handle. Things are happening too fast. I'll need time to give her a nudge.*

Eriol didn't like that last thought, but swallowed it all the same. He looked at Rodrigo and said, "Not yet."

Appendix A | Witchese Language

This language is spoken by the race of Witches. As they are a dark race, their language is very guttural, and unpleasant to the ears of humans and other beings. Even homunculi have trouble listening to it.

Phonology

The consonant inventory of Witchese is very limited, including mostly plosive and fricative consonants.

	Bilabial	Alveolar	Palatal
Stop	p b	t d	k g
Fricative		s z	ǩ ǧ

There is also a lateral alveolar [l], a post-alveolar rhotic [r], and a glottal fricative [h], which assimilates to a glottal stop after back vowels. The palatal fricatives, [ǩ] and [ǧ] are written as 'kh' and 'gh' in non-linguistic discourse.

There are five vowel sounds, corresponding to the basic vowels of English: [a], [i], [e], [o], and [u]. They however can be realised differently. [o] is often realised as English 'pot,' but after [l] may be pronounced as in 'corn.' Similarly, [e] is realised as in 'pet,' but is pronounced as 'ey' before fricatives. At the ends of words, [u] is pronounced as in Japanese (a short, unrounded back vowel – pronounce the word 'sue' without rounding the lips); within words, it is a much more rounded sound, as in English 'pool.' **[i]** and **[a]** are the same as in English.

Morphology

Witchese is a highly agglutinative language, conveying its grammatical meanings through affixes to root words. These affixes are mostly prefixes and suffixes, but infixes are known in rare occasions.

The following are noun markers.

The suffix **–i** forms the vocative case, used when invoking a name (though not necessarily referring to it as a subject of a sentence). It can sometimes be used as a topic marker. E.g. **krudi** *The Lightning*. This affix is applied before other markers.

The suffix **–su** is used in conjunction with the vocative marker to address a subordinate. E.g., **agdaisu** *You fool*.

The prefix **ub–** indicates the accusative, being the object of a sentence.

The prefix **so–** indicates a locative. E.g., **sobol** *To you*.

The verb markers are as follows:

The prefix **ak–** marks the jussive mood, indicating an order. E.g., **aktegri** *Consume it*.

The prefix **dzi–** marks the indicative mood, a statement of fact. E.g, **dziadazk** *It is uniting*.

The prefix **so–** marks a locative. E.g., **sobol** *To you*.

The suffix **–rig** is a negation marker. **Ez ǧaktrig** *Not that brat*.

Dictionary

The following is a non-comprehensive vocabulary of Witchese.

adazk	*Verb*	Unite / Merge
agda	*Noun*	Fool / weakling / easy target
blik	*Noun*	Earth / Soil / Spiritual Strength

bol	*Pronoun*	You
ez	*Pronoun*	That one over there
ğakt	*Noun*	Boy / Imp / Waste
gtu	*Conjunction*	Similar in meaning to English 'if'
hai	*Verb*	Receive / absorb
katezo	*Verb*	Destroy / Annihilate
krud	*Noun*	Lightning / Electricity
loetu	*Verb*	Incinerate / Burn / Vaporize / Destroy
lokt	*Pronoun*	Where
oğalra	*Verb*	Disintegrate / crumble
praz	*Noun*	Box / Chest / Container
raz	*Pronoun*	We / These ones here
tegri	*Verb*	Consume / Eat / Devour
tseg	*Verb*	Invert
tuag	*Noun*	Fire / Heat
us	*Pronoun*	That one here
zlid	*Verb*	Return / give back

Concluding Notes

As we learn more of Witchese, these grammars will expand. There is still much to discover. Although the DWMA does keep extensive records, they are under lock and key. Without much cooperation between the Lee Clan, the Alchemic Regiment, and the Reaper, there is little intelligence on this language that can be shared. Until that time, we will continue our studies with what little information we have.

About the Author

Craig Stephen Cooper grew up in Wollongong, New South Wales, Australia. At a young age, he quickly developed a flare for the dramatic, an obsession with various video games, and an aptitude for expressiveness.

In response to his desire to develop video games, his parents allowed him to study software engineering under a tutor while still in primary school. At the same time, he took dance lessons after school. He later decided drama was a path better suited to his love of storytelling, and studied speech and drama during high school.

While completing a Bachelor of Computer Engineering, he underwent practical and theory examinations for an Associate Diploma of Performance Art. During his Doctor of Philosophy in Telecommunications, he taught speech and drama to primary school children. As a member of the Fellowship of Australian Writers, he has presented workshops on storytelling and poetry, drawing on his speech and drama studies.

Cooper conceived of *The AXOM* Saga while on a train from Fukuoka to Nagasaki in Japan. Under encouragement from his friends, he wrote the stories with a passion to equal his first novel, *Final Flight of the Ranegr*.

He also dabbles in video game and mobile app development.

About the Illustrator

Tessa Eden grew up upon the shores of Australia's sunny beaches, frolicking in the sand and exploring the beautiful underwater world. Her father being a software engineer, and mother an illustrator, it was natural that she would grow to combine the two, becoming a digital artist. She now spends her days painting digitally, and creating 3D animations and CGI for animation studios in Sydney.

www.ingramcontent.com/pod-product-compliance
Lightning Source LLC
Chambersburg PA
CBHW030425120726
47903CB00003B/817